Drown Before "I Do"

A Simone Simpson Mystery

Rita Smircich

Drown Before "I Do"

A Simone Simpson Mystery

Rita Smircich

Published by "I Do" LLC

Cover design by Chris Murphy: www.cmurph.com
Book design by Pamela Pitcher: pam@documentclarity.com

Paperback ISBN:978-1-7335014-2-2
Second Edition

Printed in the United States of America 2019

Author's Note:

This is a work of fiction.
Names, characters, places, and incidents either
are the products of my imagination or are used
factiously, and any resemblance to actual persons,
living or dead, business establishments, events
or locales is entirely coincidental.

Thank you to the "I Do" LLC Team. Without their help
and expertise, these books would not be possible.

Judith Marks-White, author, teacher and editor for
her continued encouragement and support.

Chris Murphy, Illustrator, for his continued
patience and creative mind.

Ed Kelly, for his love, laughs, hope, and input.

Pamela Pitcher, Layout and Design and "sushi sister"
for her creative vision.

Laurie Goldberg, proofreader, computer
wizard, friend and confidant.

And special thanks to:

Patricia Roland, Milford resident for her
written materials on Charles Island

Thomas J. Tyler
Director
State Parks and Public Outreach Division
Department of Energy & Environmental Protection

*Dedicated to the cats and dogs that are abandoned,
lost, or in need of a home.*

Special love to the cats who touched my life:
Muli & Zak
Max & Ambrose
Sophia
Schwartz
Poly
Jeter

And to the dogs who were special to me:
Freda
Nyx
Miss Sadie

*You all gave me unconditional love, never expected
anything in return other than a head rub, food,
and snuggles. You will live in my heart forever.*

Other books by Rita Smircich:

To Do Before "I Do"
Advice, Wisdom & Practical Ideas for
Organizing and Planning Your Wedding

I Killed Grandma in Utero

Simone Simpson Mystery Series:
Die Before "I Do"
See Paris Before "I Do"

$\mathcal{O}ne$

The weight of his enormous body lying on her chest made it difficult to breathe. She corkscrewed her face in order to avoid his panting hot, rancid breath. When she opened her eyes, in return, she received a slimy kiss of drool.

"Goober, get off me," Jennifer Keys ordered as she wiped her face with her fingers, movement that excited the dog even more, and produced slimy licks on her hands, face and hair. "Stop it, you ugly mutt," she commanded as she pushed him off her chest and bed.

"Shh!" came from the 'pillow-voice' next to her.

"Sorry," she apologized to Anthony Palmieri.

She whispered to the dog, "I'm up. Happy?" She flipped the covers off her body, and looked for her slippers. She found one intact, the other was nothing more than a ball of wet stuffing.

"Beast," she mumbled, giving Goober a disapproving look. His large, mournful, human-looking mahogany brown eyes said, *I love you.*

She continued to whisper, "Don't look at me like that. You're a smelly, spoiled dog."

"Babe, get that mutt out of here. I'm trying to sleep," Anthony said more of a command than a request.

"Working on it," she mumbled.

Looking at the dog, she waved her hand, commanding him to leave the room. His nails scratched the pine floors until he got his balance, and galloped down the flight of stairs.

Goober, a three-year old rescue belonged to Anthony. The dog was seventy-five pounds of undisciplined, yet lovable fluff, with the slobbering of a St. Bernard, the body of a Border Collie, the smell of dead fish, and the loyalty of a Labrador.

Jennifer walked barefoot through the beach cottage into the kitchen. She pushed the button on her Cuisinart coffee pot, and delighted in the rich aroma that filled the room. Goober whined as he pressed against the back door, anticipating the rush of fresh air on his snout. Jennifer poured herself a cup of coffee, opened the back door, and watched as the behemoth animal charged down the flight of stairs and landed ungracefully in the sand. Just as ungracefully, he scrambled up onto all four paws, and barked as he charged towards the ocean chasing a family of sandpipers.

Jennifer yelled, "Come back with breakfast." She feared that one day he'd come home with a live bluefish hanging out of his mouth.

Milford, Connecticut has over seventeen miles of shoreline, eight parks, one state park, and twenty-four playgrounds and ball fields. There are nature trails, an Audubon Society, indoor recreation facilities, fishing, boating, and the second longest town green in New England. *A piece of paradise right outside my back door,* Jennifer thought.

She sat down on the gray concrete steps. She drank her coffee and watched the sunrise while Goober chased a group of gulls floating close to shore. The birds took off, cawing, as if cursing the dog for disturbing their morning's rest. His attention turned to a family of Canada geese. He charged into the water barking at them. They, too, took flight forming a 'V' and honked obscenities at the annoying animal. Goober ran at top speed along the shoreline, stopped, and dug in the mud trying to catch a scurrying sea creature.

Meanwhile, Anthony was not able to go back to sleep. He cursed Jennifer for allowing the stupid mutt into their bedroom, and not leaving him locked in his crate all night. He got out of bed, showered and dressed.

He sauntered into the kitchen, poured a cup of coffee and drank it as he waited for an English Muffin to pop up from the toaster. He slathered the nooks and crannies with sweet butter and country-style raspberry jam. As he ate, he looked out the window and watched Jennifer as she supervised Goober. "What a sap she is," he mumbled.

After breakfast, he left the kitchen, leaving a mess for Jennifer to clean up: the toaster was plugged into the outlet; the coffee carafe had an inch of coffee inside; his dirty dish and mug sat where he left them; the counter was dotted with muffin crumbs; a knife stood tall inside the tub of butter; a teaspoon sank inside the jar of sticky jam, and a container of half and half was left uncovered.

Anthony walked outside and got into his car. A thought crossed his mind as a trace of guilt flowed through his body. *Maybe, I should give the bitch a kiss goodbye. But, then she'll want to talk . . . blah . . . blah . . . blah. The same old shit every time. When are we getting married . . . having kids?*

He decided she wasn't worth it. He started the engine, and drove towards his office, ten minutes away.

Back on the beach, Goober galloped toward Jennifer, holding a piece of driftwood in his mouth. He dropped his prize at Jennifer's feet, setting himself down in the sand. His tail wagged ferociously, his tongue dribbled salvia onto her feet, and his eyes begged for a game of catch.

"Not today, Goobs. I have to go to work." He rewarded Jennifer with a ferocious cold-water body shake. She uttered vulgarities at him as they began their climb back to the house. The dog ran ahead of Jennifer, almost knocking her over while he pushed his way into the cottage, "Sit," she ordered. She took a microfiber dog towel off the peg by the door and dried his body. "You smell like dead mussels."

When she finished drying him, he charged to his water bowl and enthusiastically drained it, splashing most of it onto the floor.

Jennifer looked around at the remains of Anthony's breakfast on the kitchen counter. A jolt of anger and resentment coursed through her. *He does this to me all the time,* she thought. *Doesn't he know I have to go to work, too? And he knows his mother is coming here today, and I'd never let her see this mess.*

She spent the next thirty seconds convincing herself that this is what life is like living with a man. Dismissing these thoughts, she began preparing the dog's breakfast. While she opened a can of dog food, Goober began his morning dance: sitting, staring, whining, yawning, and dragging his butt a few inches closer to her. Jennifer looked down at him, and he stopped. As soon as she returned to her task, he started all over again. Finally, after several rounds of butt-dragging, his body would be firmly up against Jennifer's leg.

When the food bowl hit the floor, Goober ravishingly devoured his food, most of it falling out of the bowl and onto the kitchen floor. His snout pushed aside chairs and area rugs in pursuit of finding some kibble that scooted across the floor. Jennifer went upstairs. When she finished her shower and opened the bathroom door, Goober was sitting there, waiting. He watched as she dried her hair, brushed her teeth, and dressed for work. He did not like her spike heels, they signified abandonment. As soon as she put them on, he charged back downstairs.

Back in the kitchen, she let Goober out once more to do his business. While he chased imaginary sea creatures, she got to work cleaning up Anthony's mess. Anthony drank the last remaining coffee. She contemplated making a fresh pot for her thermos, but when she looked at her watch, she realized she didn't have enough time to brew a fresh pot. She'd be forced to drink coffee sludge at work.

She wondered why Anthony couldn't say good-bye to her or to his dog. Again, she made excuses for his behavior, assuring herself he'd change after they were married. She wasn't willing to accept that Anthony was thoughtless. Instead, she built a wall, brick by brick around her heart, keeping out the negative thoughts and feelings.

Once Goober was back inside the house, she ordered him to lie down inside his crate. He obeyed her command, but gave her a pleading look. She gave his head a sturdy rub, placed a squeaky toy near his bed, and locked the crate door, promising to return by six o'clock.

"Grandma will be here at noon to take you out. Until then, be a good boy."

Goober's sad eyes and pathetic whine begged her to stay.

She got into her Range Rover and headed toward her job, fifty-six miles away in Hartford. She cursed every mile marker as she sat in bumper-to-bumper traffic. On a good day, the drive took an hour each way. She'd often work ten hours a day, and when she got home she was expected to do the food shopping, cooking, cleaning, and take care of Goober. If she didn't do these chores, they'd be living in a pig sty. Anthony's mother, Francine never trained him to be a good housekeeper, or to be a man who shared household chores.

The long drive, coupled with her anger at Anthony and with herself, festered until she was on the brink of a panic attack. She had to calm her mind and emotions. Otherwise, she'd be in danger of getting into an accident. Jennifer forced herself to alter her barrage of thoughts. Instead, she did a mental checklist of the cottage: did she clean up the breakfast dishes, make the bed, put Goober in his crate, etc. Goober . . . a sweet, annoying, lovable, and despicable beast, all rolled up into one fat dog. These thoughts were not helping, rather increasing her panic.

Tears began to form. "You can't cry," she yelled at herself. At the next roll-to-a-stop, she checked her makeup in the mirror. Fortunately, her mascara had not turned her into a raccoon, but red blotches had formed on her cheeks. "Anthony, you make me crazy."

Her thoughts turned to Anthony's mother who came every day to walk Goober. Jennifer resisted her offer, but when Francine also left prepared dinners for them, she acquiesced. The reality was, at the end of a long day at work, and an aggravating commute, the last thing Jennifer wanted to do was go home and cook for a man who grew up eating a home-prepared meal every night. On the days there weren't leftovers, Jennifer was forced to cook. She'd be happy to eat a simple, no-fuss, no-muss peanut butter and jelly sandwich for dinner. There were times her commute home would take close to two hours, if there was a major accident on the highway, or bad weather. On those nights, she stopped at the local Italian restaurant and purchased meals to bring home. Anthony didn't care who prepared his dinner. All he wanted, and expected, was a home-cooked meal that was delicious. Nothing less.

Francine also did light housekeeping, although Jennifer hated her changing their bed sheets, or doing their laundry.

"Anthony, I found my underwear refolded, and moved to another drawer. How many times have I asked you to tell your mother to stay out of my dresser? She rearranged my clothes hanging in the closet, organizing them according to color. I have my own system, and now I have to rearrange them." Jennifer was furious her personal and private space was being invaded. "The woman knows no boundaries."

"Hey, if you don't like the way she cleans, then tell her yourself," Anthony had said, dismissing Jennifer's complaint.

"I tried telling her," Jennifer said, "but she began to cry, saying I didn't appreciate all the hard work she did for us."

"Well, maybe you don't," he said siding with his mother. "It's that much less you have to do. You're always complaining how tired you are when you come home from work. If ma didn't do this stuff, it would never get done."

"Well, if you helped out every once in a while, we wouldn't need your mother here to clean up."

"Are you going to start that again?" Anthony snapped. "Drop it. I told you housework is woman's work. Besides, I don't want to hear you complaining about her leaving food. So she organized your underwear. Big deal."

"It is a big deal. How would you like it if your mother refolded your underwear?" She waited a beat, realizing what she had just said did not faze Anthony at all. "I'm going to sleep." Jennifer was annoyed by his lack of understanding. She turned off the light, ending their argument.

Her reverie was interrupted when she pulled her car into her office's parking lot. She grabbed her oversized pocketbook, leather messenger bag, and headed inside. The sound of her heels on the tile floor click-clacked, like a tune repeating itself over and over: "Get out. Get out. Get out."

She had looked for work in Milford, but there weren't any job openings in her field. She hated the commute, and the people with whom she worked, and more importantly, despised the job as Sales and Marketing Event Coordinator. She was responsible for organizing expos, creating marketing materials for new health and beauty products, and educating the regional sales force. The company promoted the importance of taking drugs for any and all ailments, as well as beauty products and injections, removing years from one's face and body. Their goal was to persuade consumers they required the very products they hawked.

Drug reps constantly flirted with Jennifer. In exchange for promoting their products, the salesmen promised her coveted seats to Broadway shows, vacation getaways, and all the recreational drugs she could desire. But she always politely declined their offers and advances.

Jennifer believed that if she didn't have a long commute and a demanding job, she wouldn't be so stressed, and wouldn't take it all out on Anthony. Instead, she was frazzled, and, as Anthony said, crabby all the time. She convinced herself that he was justified being annoyed with her, and that they needed Francine's help in order to run their household smoothly, and without strain.

When Jennifer had time to stop and listen to her heart, she accepted that she was not happy with her present situation. She tried to convince herself, *If I did this, or that, or didn't say things to upset Anthony, things would be better.* But the reality was, she had vested so much time and money into this relationship, she wasn't willing to give it up.

She wished she could return to the job she truly loved - working with Simone Simpson at "I Do" LLC, an upscale wedding planning company in Fairfield, Connecticut, where, she received a six-figure salary. She mused about how her life had changed. After several disagreements with Simone over Anthony, and being blamed for withholding life-altering information, she and Simone split their partnership.

As Jennifer stared out her office window, she recalled the evening she had told Anthony about her disagreement with Simone, and how he had encouraged her to leave the business.

"Hey babe, don't worry about her. She sounds like a stuck up bitch. Why don't you dump her, and go out on your own?"

"I can't leave. I'm committed."

"No one owns you."

"I'm a partner in the firm. I signed a non-compete contract. I can't just walk out."

"He's playing on your impulsiveness, Jen," Simone had said. Meanwhile, Anthony continued to encourage Jennifer to break away from her partner and friend, perpetuating the fantasy of being on her own, and fueling her inherent spontaneous nature. As Jennifer relived that time, she wondered, *If only I had tried to work things out with Simone . . . but then, I wouldn't be with Anthony.*

"Get out. Get out. Get out," the tune in her head continued.

Two

Nine months earlier, Jennifer Keys and Jonathan Vasquez had flown back to New York from Paris, France. They, along with Simone Simpson of "I Do" were the planners for a destination wedding for Biff Bradshaw and Barbara Kemp. The nuptials never took place due to the untimely death of a wedding party member.

Simone remained in Paris, waiting for Charlie Hamilton who arrived a few hours after Jennifer and Jonathan's departing flight. She and Charlie spent several days in Paris, explored the city of love, and then spent a week in Nice.

"I secretly wish it had been our honeymoon," Charlie had said, then added, "I know, Simone, not yet. But soon, I hope."

Anthony Palmieri sat by the plane window, Jennifer in the middle seat, and Jonathan on the aisle.

Anthony was on the connecting flight home, after spending three weeks touring Italy and visiting family in Sicily. He and Jennifer struck up a conversation which lasted the entire flight home. She told him about her job, and the unfortunate circumstances of the wedding's cancelation. Anthony claimed to have heard of the company, "I Do" and was intrigued to meet someone who planned events and weddings for the rich and famous.

The two discussed their respective backgrounds.

Jennifer said, "My family consists of my mother and my older brother, Terrance who live together on Long Island. He's an alcoholic, and is following in the footsteps of my deceased father. I blame my mother for enabling my father's alcoholism, and his eventual death from cirrhosis, and she's doing the same thing with my brother. Our relationship is strained because my mother is always asking me when I'm going to finally settle down, find a good husband, and give her grandchildren." Jennifer thought that last tidbit would be a subtle way of telling him she's single, and an opener for Anthony to reveal his relationship status.

What Jennifer didn't reveal was that her family's last name wasn't Keys, it was Keogh. Her father, Patrick was the town drunk, and his name was often in the local newspapers for fighting in saloons or at work. When she attended elementary and middle schools, Jennifer was called the "Keogh Kid." Often, she was teased by her peers, "There's the drunk's daughter." The Sisters of Perpetual Help at her elementary school said, "If your father didn't drink Satan's poison, he wouldn't be behind in tuition."

Before starting high school, Jennifer begged her mother to allow her to change her last name to Keys, to protect herself from being bullied at school. Although her mother was upset by her daughter's decision, she understood, and agreed to loan Jennifer the money for the legal costs. Jennifer got part time jobs, and over the next three years, paid back the loan. Jennifer decided that until it was absolutely necessary, there wasn't any good reason to tell Anthony her family's last name.

Anthony told Jennifer his family's history. "I have an identical twin Vinny, three sisters: Cathy, Margaret and Theresa, and my parents, Johnny and Francine. My brother still lives at home with my parents. He works at a local gas station, pumping gas and doing minor car repairs. My three sisters are married, and have kids. I have relatives who live across the street, next door, and down the street. "We sort-of own the neighborhood," Anthony joked.

Jennifer grew up with very few relatives living in the United States; most lived in Ireland. Hearing about Anthony's large extended family made her imagine what life would be surrounded by numerous relatives.

Her fantasy was interrupted when Anthony added, "I live in Milford with my dog, Goober in a cottage by the beach."

"Ever been married?" she asked.

"No. Never found the right woman," Anthony said. "You?" he asked.

"Very briefly," Jennifer answered. "Marriage didn't last longer than a few days."

Jennifer turned to look out the window. *Finally,* Jennifer thought, *I've met a clean-cut guy who wasn't married, didn't say his wife doesn't understand him, or was tangled up in a divorce, or in the middle of a custody battle.*

During their seven hour flight over the Atlantic, they talked about their mutual childhoods, jobs, and political preferences. It was obvious to both of them that they had finally met their partner in life . . . their soul mate.

I can't wait to tell Simone about Anthony, Jennifer mused. *She'll be so happy for me.*

I can't wait to tell Vinny about Jennifer, Anthony mused. *She's pretty and gullible.*

He's cute, she thought.

I wonder if she's rich, he thought.

And Jonathan slept.

Three

In Anthony Palmieri's family, given names were sacred, yet flexible. His father, Johnny was given the name Giovanni at birth, but hated having his father and grandfather's name. He was always called Johnny. Never John. He and his brother, Carmine were fifteen months apart, and could easily pass for twins. Both had strong facial features like their father's boxer's nose, cleft chin, uneven-sized ears, and closely-set brown eyes. Both had prominent receding hairlines. Johnny's remaining hair was styled into a buzz cut. Carmine shaved his head.

Anthony's mother was Francine. Never Fran, Franny, or Annie. Cathy was Catherine, a birth name rarely said, whereas Margaret and Theresa proudly used their given names. Vinny was Vincent Michael, a name only used when he was in trouble. Finally, Anthony was Anthony (pronounced Ant-knee), Ant, or Anthony Michael, and like his twin, his full name was used only when he was in trouble. He hated the nickname, Tony because when he was a young boy someone told him that mothers in Sicily wrote, TO NY on their kid's foreheads before sending them on the boat headed to the United States.

Life in the Palmieri household was orderly. It ran like a well-oiled engine, under the force and demands of the disciplinarian, Francine. She often portrayed the dumb and underappreciated housewife, but she was extremely shrewd, and didn't let anything get past her. Her 5'4" frame was compact and wide from years of eating too much of her homemade lasagna, including the remains left behind on the dishes of her family. She had brown eyes with dark circles that observed everything and everyone. Her hair was dyed jet black and cut short.

Her upper lip and chin displayed dark hairs which she refused to have waxed. Occasionally, her daughter Cathy would pluck the hairs on her chin, or apply Nair to her upper lip. But when it came to Francine taking care of her own personal hygiene of her face, she expected the help from her daughters. Her son-in-law, Cathy's husband, considered Francine's hair-plucking demands mentally sick, disgusting, and disturbing.

"Give her the name of an esthetician," Francine's son-in-law would tell his wife.

"I did. So did Margaret. But she'd rather have us do it for her. Her thinking is why should she pay a young chippy money to remove the hair, when she can get it done for free?"

"And you don't find this a little disturbing?" he'd ask.

"I know . . . I know . . . but she does so much for us. It's the least I can do for her."

Cathy's husband would just shake his head in disbelief.

When they were children, Anthony and his identical twin Vinny were inseparable, and always dressed alike. Francine claimed they were to be the next Wrigley's Doublemint Twins. As they grew they developed the same mannerisms, mimicking each other's actions. When one cried or laughed, the other followed suit. They were mirror images of each other. Anthony was left-handed, and Vinny was right-handed.

Together they played jokes on their teachers, girlfriends, and family members. Anthony found math an easy subject, and Vinny was drawn to creative writing. Frequently, they'd switch classes, took tests for each other, and did the other's homework. The teachers were unsuccessful keeping them in separate classrooms. They did everything possible to look the same, kept to a strict diet and focused on keeping their bodies in similar shape.

"When are you boys going to grow up?" their father Johnny would ask. "You two think you're still toddlers, dressing alike. You're in high school for Christ's sake. Act your age!"

"Leave them alone," Francine told her husband, indulging the boys with her approval. "It's cute."

"It ain't cute. It's sick," he replied angrily. He left for work feeling disgust at his wife who mollycoddled the boys.

Now, at thirty, they had never given up their immature thinking or antics.

Francine kept the house spotless. She did all the cooking, tended the garden, and made sure everyone, especially the men, were well fed, and always had clean ironed clothes to wear.

Until the day Anthony moved out and got his own place, Francine picked up his wet towels from the bathroom floor, made his bed, and washed his breakfast cups and dishes.

In the evening, a home-cooked meal was presented to the family. Afterwards, Francine did all the cleanup. "Cleanliness is next to godliness," she'd tell her family. She'd repeat this mantra to herself while she cleared the kitchen table, loaded the dishwasher, scrubbed the pots and pans, wiped down the stove, and washed the linoleum floor at 11:30 at night, while everyone else was asleep.

During the day, she washed her family's clothes, folded them, and put them back where they belonged. She would mend their clothes, polish their shoes, and organize their bureaus and closets. The men did not do any household chores. And since her daughters were married, and running their own households, she had to do all the housework herself.

Screaming in Italian, and slamming doors were the everyday sounds in the Palmieri household. Cheeks were pinched, along with "Faccia bella!" Francine gave hugs and cookies to her grandchildren, along with the question, "Who loves her little grandson?" Leaving the child to answer this confusing question: *Who loves me? Is it grandma with a cookie in her hand? Or, the lady down the street who lets me play with her puppy?* Actual feelings and loving words were avoided and sidetracked, adding to the dysfunction of the family.

Through the noise and anger, positive feelings weren't discussed or displayed. No one said, "I love you," or "I'm so proud of you." Instead, "What do you want, a medal?" was the accolade for a high achievement in school or at work.

Secrets were communion in the Palmieri family. Everyone received them, and everyone kept them. When Francine saw her brother-in-law, Carmine in the movie theatre with a woman who wasn't his wife, Tara, she said nothing. When she saw her son with another woman, and not his girlfriend, Angie, she said nothing. She kept these secrets vaulted in her heart, and only released them in the confessional box. The pastor of her church could write volumes about the Palmieri family's indiscretions, fights and grudges.

Francine never told her husband anything she observed or overheard. He didn't need, or want, to know. She was the matriarch of the family, a burden she wore like a scarlet letter. Her husband, Johnny, worked hard, and when he came home, he didn't want to hear about the trials and tribulations of the day. "Handle it," was his standard response.

Anthony's maternal grandparents lived two houses away with an unmarried daughter who was their caretaker. Another maternal aunt lived three blocks away. She, her husband, and five kids were frequent visitors to Johnny's house. Francine's first cousin, his wife, and three children, lived across the street. They too were frequent visitors. On average, Sunday dinner at Johnny and Francine's table would range from seven to twenty-seven people, devouring Francine's world famous spaghetti and meatballs. Famous, if only in her mind.

The only Palmieri family members missing were Johnny's brother and his family. They were never to cross Johnny and Francine's threshold.

Four

Carmine and Tara Palmieri lived in the house next door, to the right of Johnny and Francine. Carmine was Johnny's younger brother. Their father, Giovanni owned a successful plumbing and heating company, where the two boys worked since they were teenagers. Both men became licensed plumbers, and were treated just like the other licensed workers at their father's company.

While working for his father, Carmine skimmed money off invoices. If a customer paid a bill with cash after a service call, Carmine gave them a completed paid invoice, but back in his truck, he'd create a new invoice. He changed the service call to a minor repair, lowered the charges, and kept the difference. Then, he submitted the lower amount to the receptionist as 'paid in full.'

Keeping with tradition of the Palmieri family, Carmine kept secrets too. He told select customers he could do their job at a cheaper rate if they hired him privately, and paid cash. Several customers, who were struggling to keep their businesses going during a difficult economy, were receptive to this offer.

Their father's business was struggling as well. Big box stores opened in close proximity to his company. A new kitchen faucet could be purchased for 30% less at Home Depot, or Lowes, with a greater selection than at Giovanni's store.

"I need to change my business plan," he told his accountant. "I think the company needs to move into new construction, instead of individual jobs. Otherwise, I'm going to be forced to close."

"You have a great business, Giovanni. I don't understand why you're losing money month after month, when your margins are close to 60%," Bobby, the CPA said. "Something's not right," he added.

Giovanni learned about Carmine's scheme simply by accident. A customer came into the shop while Carmine and Johnny were out in the field. He complained that a part Carmine had ordered over a month ago, was never delivered. The father looked through old invoices, found the one related to the job, and discovered the part was not noted on the invoice.

"It shows you only needed a new washer, not a diverter valve."

"He charged me for it," said the customer.

"It only shows a washer, and the charge was $50."

"I paid him $450 for a new shower diverter."

"I don't mean to disagree with you, Andy, but are you sure you ordered it through Carmine?"

"I'm sure. You know, Giovanni, that I only do business with you. I have for over twenty years."

"How did you pay for the part?"

"I paid cash," replied Andy.

"I'm sure there's a mix up. I apologize for the confusion. I'll order a new part for you, free of charge, and have Johnny install it for you as soon as it comes in. Again, I'm sorry for the inconvenience."

The men shook hands, "Thank you for your continued business, Andy. I promise, I'll take care of this as soon as possible." Warm wishes were exchanged.

Giovanni spent the next few days going through old invoices. He had to do this after hours, as he suspected his secretary and Carmine were fooling around outside of work, and outside of their marriages.

On the second night of going through old invoices, Giovanni discovered the inconsistency of the numerical orders in Carmine's invoice books. And this answered why, on occasion, supplies went missing from their stockroom. He wondered if Carmine had been doing jobs on the side as well, and using his inventory. To his dismay, he discovered this had gone on for several years.

The father made calls to long-standing customers, feigning he was calling about quality control. But he was actually backtracking to see who paid cash, and if the amounts matched the date of the invoice. In the instances when the customer paid cash, there was a skip in the invoice numbers. Giovanni realized that Carmine was giving the customer a paid invoice showing what they had paid in cash, but then privately, would tear up that numbered invoice, and create another invoice, logging a lower charge. Carmine was keeping the difference. He wondered if his secretary knew about this, and in addition, was receiving hush money from Carmine.

Giovanni didn't say anything to his son, but going forward he reviewed Carmine's jobs, compared invoice numbers, and the inventory in the warehouse. He felt like an old fool. He never suspected his son would steal from him. All of Johnny's jobs were precise, as well as his other workers. The job description, amount, and equipment were exact, with no dubious actions.

"Bobby, can we meet in your office?" Giovanni asked his accountant. "I have some information I'd like to share with you. I'm also bringing along my attorney."

The accountant and attorney reviewed Giovanni's findings. "He should be arrested," the attorney said.

"No, I can't do that to my son, although he deserves to be put in jail for what he's done to me, and to my business." The old man shook his head feeling defeated and embarrassed. "I have another plan, which he discussed in great detail with the two professionals."

Giovanni had been diagnosed with lung cancer six months before. He told no one, not even his wife, Joyce. "I ain't doing nothing about it, doc. I've had a good life."

Fifteen months later, Giovanni Palmieri was dead.

At the reading of his will, it stipulated that his son, Giovanni, would inherit the business. A sealed envelope was given to his son, with the handwritten words on the front: *Read in private.* Inside, the letter said: *Johnny, you are creative, smart, and have a pulse on the future markets. I trust you. You never cheated me. Learn what you can from others in the business. If you find the competition too much from the big stores, sell the business. Your loving father, Giovanni.*

The attorney read, "And to my son, Carmelino, I leave him $1.00, and I mean $1.00. Nothing more. My son, Carmelino, my flesh and blood, stole from me. I know. I saw. He is never to step foot into the business again. I leave everything to my son, Giovanni."

While they worked for their father, the brothers were paid the same amount, a fair salary rate; possibly higher than the average plumber. Their father carried the full cost of doing business: insurance, staff, overhead, inventory, and all the other expenses related to running a business. And now, Johnny was faced with this responsibility and burden.

Carmine and Tara lived far above their means. She didn't work, unless you considered the propensity for shopping a job. Her motto was: *you don't know you need it, until you see it.*

The couple had money for expensive vacations, designer clothes, and money for tutors for their daughter, Veronica. They spent tens of thousands of dollars on tuition to send her to private schools. Carmine let Tara run the household. He handed over his paycheck to his wife, and added a percentage of what he skimmed off. He knew that if he gave her all of his extra cash, she'd spend it on a new outfit.

Johnny, on the other hand, held the purse strings. He gave Francine a weekly allowance, and frequently warned her about hanging out with Tara for fear she would develop her spending habits. Francine resented Johnny's financial hold on her, but when she seriously thought about it, he was right. "Don't try to keep up with the Joneses," he'd say. Tara would coax her sister-in-law into buying something expensive, and suggested she hide it in the trunk of her car until Johnny wasn't home. This happened two times, but when Francine ran out of money to purchase groceries, she knew she could never keep up with Tara's extravagant tastes and lifestyle.

After leaving the attorney's office, the two brothers argued about the distribution of wealth. Johnny suspected his brother had his hand in the till, but turned a blind eye, not wanting to snoop or search for proof. He kept his suspicions to himself, and never said anything to his father. Regardless of Johnny's innocence, Carmine accused his brother of fabricating a scenario so that his share of the business would be taken away from him.

Carmine demanded, "Now what am I going to do for work?"

"Stay at the company for the next six months. I'll give you some jobs and pay you cash so the lawyer doesn't find out. Obviously, dad will never know. Meanwhile, you can look for another job."

Carmine was mule-headed, like their father, and refused his brother's help. "I don't want any of your sympathy," snapped Carmine. "I'd rather starve than take anything from you. I'm no charity case, dear brother."

Johnny was inquisitive and asked his brother, "*Were* you stealing from dad? I never said anything to him to make him suspicious, but he must have discovered something to make him take you out of the will."

"I'm not answering that," Carmine snapped. "You must have done something, or said something to make him think I took money from the miser. Well, I hope you're happy now. You finally got what you wanted. I never want to see or talk to you again."

"Carmine, if you were stealing, you know that dad would have found out sooner or later." Johnny repeated, "I suspected you were playing around with invoices. I never looked for proof, nor did I ever say anything to dad."

Johnny continued, "I often wondered how you had extra money for extravagant things, like trips to Europe and new cars. Tara didn't work, but could afford to wear Hermes scarfs and carry a Louis Vuitton handbag."

"Go to hell," Carmine yelled at his brother. "I'm not like you, paying to keep your entitled spoiled twins out of jail, paying off judges, and the cops."

Johnny thought his "donations" to the PAL, and to the elected local officials were kept private. Apparently, not.

"I know what goes on in your household, too. Don't ever question how I spend my money. And don't ever talk to me again."

"But Carmine . . ."

His brother got into his truck and sped away, leaving Johnny speechless. From that day forward, the two brothers never spoke to each other again.

Five

At one time, Francine and Tara Palmieri were close, frequently spending time together shopping, going out for lunch, to the movies, or babysitting for each other's kids. They shared appliances rarely used: a crock pot, an immersion blender, a rice cooker, asparagus and artichoke steamers, and a bread maker. They were in and out of each other's homes regularly, especially when one needed an egg, an onion, or flour.

Often, when they went clothes shopping, they'd purchase the same outfit. Tara was a petite size two, and Francine was full-figured, a squeeze-into-size eighteen. It wasn't often that Francine looked better than Tara in the same outfit.

Francine yearned to be like her sister-in-law: slim, in shape, and great looking in anything she put on. Tara had short straight hair, the color of clarified butter. Her blue eyes dominated her face, and when she wore light summer colors, her eyes would look like two lights coming towards you. She had a wardrobe that any woman would envy, with expensive handbags, shoes and other accessories. Francine, like her husband, questioned where the money came from, but she assumed Tara got an inheritance from her parents, whom she spoke of as well-established in life.

When Tara became a grandmother, she turned to Francine for advice on how to baby-proof her house. Since Francine had over a decade of experience with grandkids, she was a wealth of information and she had strong opinions. Tara inquired about the latest gadgets, clothing, glass vs. plastic bottles, and how grandparents were raising grandkids these days. "What about baby monitors?" Tara asked Francine.

"I have an extra one," Francine said. Theresa and Cathy each got two at their baby showers. I'll give you one. It's great when your granddaughter sleeps over so you can watch your shows."

Tara thought, *There she goes again about her soap operas, and reality TV. If she went for a walk or exercised, that dress wouldn't look like a muumuu on her.*

When the fallout happened after their father-in-law died, and the brothers were no longer speaking to each other, the women were forbidden to be friends. Francine, more than Tara felt the impact of the lost friendship. Tara still went about her shopping adventures, albeit alone or with a new friend. Francine spent more time cleaning and cooking for her married daughters, and discovered her love of reality shows with *The Real Housewives* series, both national and international versions. Her obsession grew to include *Say Yes to the Dress, Bridezillas,* and a slew of other reality TV shows.

Francine lived in a world of denial and fantasy. She believed her children could do nothing wrong. Even when she witnessed bad behavior, she made excuses for them, turning a blind eye to their selfish and nasty conduct. In her mind, her life was perfect, unlike the lives of the housewives or brides on TV, where everyone seemed to have drama, heartache and unhappiness, no matter how rich they were. When there was a serious tragedy with a TV reality housewife, Francine congratulated herself on running a peaceful home filled with harmony and love.

Once, when Veronica was visiting her mother, the subject of the Palmieri family next door came up in conversation. Tara said, "My sister-in-law thinks her family is perfect. If anyone knew what really went on in that house, they'd be shocked."

"What do you mean, mom?" Veronica asked.

"When Francine and I went shopping she'd bitch about your Uncle Johnny. She told me things about him that would make him furious. I just listened."

"Like what?"

"Never you mind," Tara told her daughter. "Let's just say, it ain't all peaches and cream over there. She watches those soap operas and someone else's drama to convince herself she has a normal and happy life. What a joke."

Running into each other was uncomfortable, so both women began shopping at different supermarkets and dry cleaners. When, by accident, they did run into each other, they were cordial with forced politeness. They didn't go out of their way to make conversation, or sneak away for lunch, for fear one of their husbands would find out. No, their friendship fizzled quickly, with only minor regret.

For years, Tara had felt Francine walked in her shadow, trying to dress and act like her. Francine, now that her sister-in-law was out of the picture, had to find her own identity. And that identity she found was someone who cooked, ate, and watched soap operas all day. Conversely, Tara made new shopping purchases, ate smaller portions, and exercised daily.

Six

Carmine secured a job working as a plumber for a competitor, but his take-home pay wasn't nearly as much as when he worked for his father, and skimmed money. He tried stealing from his new boss, and offered to do side-jobs for customers. Word got back to his employer, and he was quickly fired. Of course Carmine blamed his brother, claiming Johnny told his new boss to "watch out" for his antics. But this wasn't true.

Carmine's next job was at a big box hardware store, but was fired after a week. He was caught on the security camera stealing a generator, which he later sold to a friend. Eventually, Carmine got work at a local sporting goods store. He vowed to never steal again, or more to the point, never to get caught again.

Using his employee discount, he purchased six baseball bats, a dozen softballs, two pairs of cleats, and sports gloves, all of which he kept stored in an army duffle bag in the garage. He joined the company's softball team, and found a new sense of happiness and purpose by surrounding himself with people other than his brother and his family. *I was never good enough for my older brother - never appreciated. Now, I don't have to look for his approval.*

Carmine found an outlet where he could release his pent-up anger, smashing a softball over the left field fence. He quickly became the much sought-after team player. If he had found his love of softball earlier in his life, maybe he could have gone professional. "What-if's" plagued Carmine since he was a young teen. He imagined his older brother was better than him, faster and stronger, and often quelled his dreams of being successful. These thoughts were demons he could never overcome.

The two brothers continued to live side by side, with a six-foot fence making them good neighbors. Grudges were held for generations. It was a Palmieri tradition.

Carmine and Tara's daughter, Veronica, came to visit her parents several times a week. When she and her husband had a fight, she'd stay for weeks at a time, bringing her toddler with her. Carmine found the child annoying and an intrusion. When he got home from work, he wanted a beer, a home-cooked meal, and peace and quiet. Sometimes when Veronica was at the house, he'd call Tara and say he had to work late, or participate in a softball game. Instead, he'd go to a local tavern, consume his fill of bar food and beer, and arrive home after midnight, knowing his wife, daughter and granddaughter were asleep.

"Carmine, why did you stay out so late?" Tara asked her husband one Saturday morning. He was sitting at the kitchen table drinking his third cup of coffee, and nursing a hangover. "Veronica thinks you don't want to be around her and the baby."

"I don't," he said flatly.

"That's not nice. She's your only daughter and your only grand-daughter. You should spend some time with them."

"They're always here. Doesn't she know how to work out her problems with her husband? She shouldn't run home to her mommy whenever they have a fight. She needs to stay in her own home, and get over it."

Tara stared at her husband of thirty years with a look of contempt. There were many times she wished she had gone home to her parents, never to return to this man, who was mean-spirited and selfish.

"If Veronica and Eric get a divorce, I want to invite her to move back home," Tara said as she stirred skim milk into her coffee.

"Oh no, you won't. I don't want no little twit running around this house screaming and crying. I ain't changing no diapers, or doing midnight feedings. I did that when Veronica was a baby. I ain't doing it again. End of subject. Tell her to get her own apartment. If you want to babysit her during the day, that's your business. Just don't expect me to put up with her, or her crying baby."

Carmine took his dish of scrambled eggs and toast, and shoved his breakfast down the garbage disposal. He walked out of the kitchen, picked up a bat and left the house.

"Animal," Tara shouted after him.

She called up to Veronica, "Can you come down here? I need to talk to you."

Veronica was dressed in a cotton nightgown, sans bra. Her eyes showed signs of mascara that wasn't removed the night before, and her hair was a large mass of unruly curls on top of her head. She looked twenty years older than her age. *No wonder her husband was cheating on her,* Tara thought. Unkind thoughts, she acknowledged, but it seemed her daughter didn't try to make herself presentable.

She was holding baby Juliet in her arms. The child had been crying, and she, too, had dark circles under her eyes from lack of sleep. Her hair was matted down from sweat. The two of them looked like refugees.

Tara looked at the pathetic pair and announced, "I'm going for my morning jog. I'll be back in forty minutes." Then she continued, "Veronica, I think you need to go back home to Eric. It's not healthy for your marriage to leave every time you have a fight. You need to work things out between the two of you. Besides, you're not setting a good example for the baby. She needs to see that her parents can solve their problems."

"I can't believe what you're saying." Veronica began crying. Juliet seeing her mother upset, began to cry, too. "See what you did," she shouted at her mother. "It's all your fault."

"Ah . . ." but Tara never finished her sentence. Veronica ran back upstairs screaming that she hated her mother.

Tara walked out the door hoping that her daughter and grand-daughter would be gone when she got back home. *She needs to grow up,*

Tara thought. *I've babied her for too many years. She's a grown woman and needs to take responsibility for her actions. Maybe Carmine is right,* though she'd never tell him.

While Carmine smacked baseballs to release his frustrations, Tara pounded the pavement, smashing her feelings of guilt and uncertainty.

Meanwhile, next door the Palmieri twins whispered about their cousin, and her dependency on her parents. They heard her screaming at her mother through the open windows.

"The mental case is back. Again. Doesn't she ever go home?" Anthony said, as he stood by the kitchen sink that overlooked his relative's home. "She's always here with her bratty little kid."

"Yeah, it seems she's at her parent's house, more than her own," Vinny agreed, as he ate the last of a ham and cheese sandwich his mother made for him.

"Be nice," Francine scolded her sons. "She can't help it if she's a little slow. Be respectful to Veronica and her parents. After all, they're blood."

"Dad wouldn't be happy to hear you defending them," Anthony responded.

"What your father doesn't know won't hurt him," Francine countered.

Seven

Since their first meeting, Jennifer spent most nights at Anthony's cottage in Devon, a charming section of Milford. Within three months, and Anthony's promises of a future life together, she moved in full time. She kept her apartment in Fairfield, and used it primarily as a closet for her extensive wardrobe and shoes. Or when Anthony had his buddies over for a night of drinking and playing poker. On those nights, she and Goober went to her apartment, away from the partying, foul language, and cigar smoke. She turned a blind eye to Anthony's behavior on the excuse she needed a good night's sleep.

"It's just once in a while, babe," he promised. "Like, every three months."

"We've been together for three months, Anthony, and this is the fifth time your buddies came, and stayed overnight. Can't they go to one of the other guy's houses?"

"Their wives aren't like you, babe. They don't understand that we guys work hard all week, and just want to blow off steam. It's not like we're going out to bars and gambling," Anthony said, justifying his actions.

"Okay," she agreed. "But I don't want to have to clean up after all of you when I come back in the morning."

Anthony vowed, "Don't worry, babe. I'll clean up."

But he never did. While he slept off a hangover, Jennifer would throw out ashtrays of cigarettes, cigars, left over food, and placed dozens of beer and liquor bottles in the recycle bin. Then she'd run the vacuum, clean the kitchen, and mumble to herself, "This will change once we're married."

Sometimes, those evenings turned into a wild party, featuring poker tournaments, excessive drinking, and doing recreational drugs. Often, Fran the Can, as Anthony's brother Vinny called her, joined in the fun. After her late-night shift at *The Cat's Meow,* she'd sneak in, away from nosy neighbors' eyes. She'd perform one of her acts, leaving with a G-string filled with money.

Jennifer never suspected, or admitted that Anthony cheated on her. *He's never given me a reason not to trust him,* she convinced herself. Except for the boys' nights, he came home every evening, professed his love for her, and was attentive to all her physical needs.

Eight

Three years ago, during one of Francine's famous-family Sunday dinner's, Aunt Carmella asked the twins, "Isn't it time you two got your own places? How old are you now? When are you going to marry nice Italian girls and start families?"

They did not answer their aunt's questions about marriage and children. Their eyes went from their aunt, to their mother, back to their aunt.

"They'll move when they're ready," Francine quickly said, giving her sister a 'none of your business' look. Francine loved having her sons living at home, playing the role of mother, cook and bottle washer. These were her babies. It didn't matter how old they were, she still considered them her little boys.

Anthony thought about what his aunt had said. In their so-called bachelor pad in the basement, the boys discussed the idea of moving out.

"Vin, I'm thinking maybe Aunt Carmella is right. Maybe we should move out and get a place of our own. I'm tired of our relatives watching and scrutinizing our every move.

"Nah, I like it here," his twin responded. "Yeah, it's tough juggling when one of us has a girl over . . . who has to go out for a few hours, and stuff . . . but I ain't going to start cleaning or cooking.

"Ma can still do that for us. I'm sure she'll beg us to do the housework," Anthony said, having the solution to their problems.

"Besides," added Vinny, "I don't have money to move out. I've only got that job at the gas station, and that pays zilch. So until I get a job with benefits, I'm staying here."

"I think I'm going to start looking," Anthony said.

Anthony reflected back on a story he read in Cosmo Magazine at his dentist's waiting room. He thought he'd see photos of girls in skimpy bikinis, or Victoria's Secret ads. There was a fair share of models, but his eyes were drawn to an article entitled, *Moving Out for the Wrong Reasons*. The story stated that, although things have changed in the job market with women's salaries now close to men's, many women still felt they could not make it on their own without a second income. Women were being hired in higher-paying positions, but the cost of living was still too high for women to live on their own. They needed a roommate to share expenses, or a husband to support them.

The article further said: *don't go from being someone's daughter, to someone's wife, to someone's mother without first knowing who you are.*

Anthony thought that was very insightful. He saw his three sisters, and his next door cousin go directly from their parents' home to being married. And shortly afterwards, having kids. His sisters often complained they never had time for themselves, and now that they were getting older, they didn't like the same things they did in their twenties. His sisters didn't go to college, though many of the women in their neighborhoods had college degrees, good jobs, and a life away from diapers.

Anthony agreed with Aunt Carmella: maybe it was time to move out and find a place of his own. He fantasized what it would be like, to have parties and girls over whenever he wanted.

Conversely, Vinny didn't care what family members said. He knew that at his age he should be living on his own. But he had a good thing going, his mother cooked, cleaned, and did his laundry. He had Angie, a loyal and long-time girlfriend, plus Joanie, a lover who shared his bed when her abusive husband got drunk and passed out.

Shortly after their discussion, Anthony told his brother that he found a place on the beach in Devon. "Want to move in with me, bro? It's got two bedrooms."

Vinny thought about it, and said he couldn't afford to share the cost. Even splitting everything, he couldn't make it on his salary.

"Thanks, Ant, but I have to save for my own place. I'm thinking Aunt Carmella might be right. I should be thinking about getting married and starting a family."

Anthony pondered his brother's words. "Well, I ain't got no girl right now. Maybe when I find a rich one, I'll think about getting married."

The two brothers slapped a high five.

To prove Anthony's point, after he moved into the small cottage by the beach, he asked his mother, "Ma, do you know a woman who can clean for me? Maybe one of your Canasta friends has a cleaning lady they'd share."

Francine's eyes lit up. "Not to worry, Ant," she assured her son. "I'll come by twice a week and clean for you. You just concentrate on work, and enjoying yourself. You're young – have fun."

So, two times a week Francine Palmieri went to Anthony's cottage, and brought cooked meals with post-it notes with heating instructions.

After Anthony started dating Jennifer, and she was a regular at his cottage, Francine would stop by more frequently. She used Goober as the excuse, "The dog needs frequent walks." But Anthony's mother just wanted to snoop.

After Jennifer moved into his cottage full time, his mother was miffed that she had been replaced. Jennifer was equally annoyed she replaced Anthony's mother. At first, Jennifer thought Anthony was just a slob, leaving his bathroom towels on the floor, and breakfast dishes on the table. But when his breakfast dishes and coffee mug were left on the table after every breakfast, and his dinner dishes were left on the dining room table after every meal, Jennifer started to feel more like his maid than his partner.

When Francine arrived at the cottage, she would immediately grab a load of clothes from the laundry basket, and put them into wash. Then she'd release Goober from his crate, and in his excitement, he'd jump on her, and beg for a head rub and kisses.

"You smell," Francine once said to the dog. "Doesn't she ever give you a bath?" At the word 'bath' Goober ran back into his crate, cowering in the corner.

"Get out here, you stupid dog. I'm not giving you a bath." A repeat of the forbidden word was met with howls of anguish from Goober.

"For Christ's sake," she said annoyed.

She grabbed his leash, and vowed to herself not to say the dreaded word 'bath' again. "Come on, let's go for a walk with grandma."

Goober, not fully trusting Francine, slowly lifted his body and walked to the opening of the crate. He kept his head and front paws outside, and the rest of his body inside, ready to bolt back to the corner if she uttered that profanity again.

Francine slipped the leash around his neck, and tugged him along. After several tries her patience wore thin. He was a strong dog and no amount of pulling was going to get him out of the crate. The animal had a mind of his own, and rarely listens to a command given by her. He listened to Jennifer as she was the supplier of his food, water, kisses, and runs on the beach.

I have no choice, she decided and gave him a treat. Anthony told his mother that Goober only got a treat after a walk. But she was desperate. She wasn't going to tug at him all day. After he ate the treat, he got up and walked out of the crate.

Goober licked her hand as a thank you, and followed her out the front door for a good sniffing and leg lifting of every tree in the neighborhood.

One time when she came to walk him, Francine accidently left the front door opened. Before she could leash him, Goober bolted out the front door, and took off running from one yard to the next. He found his way to the beach and chased anything that moved. He kicked up sand onto sun worshipers, and frightened little children wading at the shoreline. It took Francine over an hour to corral him back into the house.

The result was angry beachgoers who filed a report with Animal Control and the police. Anthony received a $50 fine for Goober being off leash, and another $50 ticket for his rambunctious behavior. Anthony was furious with his mother, but knew if he yelled at her, he'd have to get a real dog walker who would charge him $50 every visit. He told her about the tickets, as calmly as he could. Francine promised she would never leave the front door open again.

After their morning walk, Francine gave Goober a treat, and she got about her chores. The dog would find a sunny spot and sleep while Francine tidied up, did laundry, and ran the dishwasher . . . and her fair share of snooping.

Francine felt entitled to know what was going on in their private lives. Once, she counted how many empty condom packets she found, and looked in Jennifer's nightstand for anything relating to their sex life.

Francine didn't understand limitations, nor would accept them even if she was told to mind her own business. One time, Anthony found his supply of condoms reorganized. He knew his mother had gone through the dresser, and the following week, he brought up the subject.

"Ma," he whispered, while he stood towering over her as she stirred a pot of pasta, "did you go through my dresser and reorganize my condoms?"

Francine didn't hesitate. She straightened her back, looked Anthony in the eyes, and with all sincerity answered, "Yes, I did. I want to be sure you're being satisfied. Jennifer is always too busy to cook for you, or do housework. I just want to be sure she's not too busy for . . . well, you know . . . you. I want you to be happy and satisfied."

Anthony didn't know how to respond to this statement. After a few moments, he said, "Thanks, ma, I'm perfectly attended to. Please stay out of my nightstand."

The conversation gave him the creeps.

Mother and son never spoke of the subject again. Francine never reorganized the condoms . . . well, not so Anthony could tell, but kept a precise inventory.

She had a hold on him, deeper than anyone could imagine.

Nine

"Anthony, we need to talk," Jennifer said one evening while eating dinner and watching TV. She was going to attempt to bring up the subject of shared responsibilities.

"Yeah, what's up babe?" he asked without taking his eyes off the Yankee game.

"We need to discuss a few things."

"Go ahead," he said, his mouth full of his mother's homemade eggplant parmigiana, left earlier that day in their refrigerator.

"What are you blind? Stupid ump," he shouted at the TV. "Check the tape. Check the tape." Anthony continued to shovel food in his mouth as he yelled at the screen.

"Anthony, can we please talk?" Her patience was starting to wear thin.

"Yeah, at the end of this inning," he said, as he shouted obscenities at the ballplayers.

Jennifer finished her dinner in silence, put her dirty dishes in the dishwasher, and took Goober for his evening walk through the neighborhood. It wasn't until thirty minutes later that Anthony came out looking for her. Not finding her, he returned to the ballgame.

When she returned, Anthony asked, "Babe, what's up?"

"Anthony, I feel you've asked me to move in with you just so I could replace your mother."

"Whoa!" Anthony immediately got defensive.

"I didn't say I *was* your mother. I said, *take* your mother's place by cleaning up after you, taking care of the dog, and all the other chores. I need you to help around the house. Your mother shouldn't be coming here taking care of you as if you were a little boy."

She added, "It's not fair that you leave your towels on the floor, and dishes on the table. Why do I have to do all of that? If I didn't clean up after you, and left everything for your mother to do when she came to walk Goober, she'd have something else to dislike about me."

Out of the corner of his eye, he continued to watch the game.

"Are you listening to me?"

"Yeah, babe, I am. Can't we talk about this after the game? The bases are loaded and it's the bottom of the ninth."

"We'll talk later," she mumbled, finally giving up.

She cleaned off the stove, washed Francine's Pyrex dish, and placed it on the kitchen table along with a note: *Thank you- it was delicious.*

When the game was over, Anthony snuggled up behind her. "What's up, babe? You seem upset. Is there something I did?"

She turned and stared at him. His dark brown eyes with black flecks made her swoon. But she had to stay strong, so she forged ahead and said, "We've been living together for over seven months. And every time I bring up the subject of marriage, you always have an excuse. I feel as if you asked me to move in with you so that you have someone to take care of Goober, and clean up after you."

At the sound of his name, Goober jumped up from his resting place and charged towards Jennifer, looking at her with admiration and unconditional love. She rubbed his head, her heart melting from his affection for her.

Anthony gave Jennifer his favorite frown, and tried imitating a little boy who was being scolded. He pulled her into his arms and kissed her passionately. "Now, that's something I don't do with my mother." He kissed her again, moving his hand under her blouse and fondling her breast.

"Anthony, not now," she managed to say breaking away from his embrace. "You're acting like a child."

She walked back into the family room. Anthony's dirty dishes and wine glass were still where he left them. He saw her looking at the table.

"I think you have to teach this boy a lesson. A real *hard* lesson," he teased, as he grabbed her and began kissing her again. Annoyed, she pushed him away.

"Stop it. Your poor-little-boy act isn't going to work on me this time. I'm really annoyed, Anthony."

She turned away from him and began to clean off the table. Anthony went into the kitchen, got a beer from the refrigerator, and plopped down on the sofa to watch the post-game show.

Yes, she thought, *I am his mother, but this will change once we're married.*

Through all of this abuse, she stayed, convincing herself that he was 'the one' for her. Or, was she staying with Anthony in order to spite Simone? She chastised me for getting involved with Anthony, so soon after meeting him. But she had never met him. Who was she to say he wasn't good for me?

For the next several months, Jennifer continued to spend time between Anthony's cottage, and her apartment during poker nights. When Anthony's lease was up for renewal, the landlord told him he wanted them out. The dog had chewed up the kitchen cabinets, the molding, and the neighbors complained about the loud parties on weekends. He gave Anthony a generous three months' notice to find another place.

Anthony and Goober moved back to his parents' home. They now shared Vinny's space in the basement. Jennifer moved back to her Fairfield apartment.

His mother was very strict about girlfriends living with her sons. "You're not married, you don't live together under my roof."

She wasn't fond of Goober, either. It was quite different going to Anthony's house to walk the dog, but she didn't like him living in her home all the time. Often, she confined him inside his crate in the basement for hours at a time, while Anthony was at work. Goober enjoyed running through her home, knocking over anything within tail height. She'd yell obscenities at the dog, and scream at Anthony, "Get that mutt out of my kitchen!"

Anthony and his dog stayed at Jennifer's studio apartment on weekends, but every surface was cluttered with clothes, dozens of pairs of designer shoes, handbags, accessories, makeup, and jewelry. Pets, especially a mammoth-sized dog like Goober, were not permitted by the landlord, except for an occasional weekend visit. Jennifer and Anthony could never leave Goober unattended in her apartment for fear he'd eat one of her Jimmy Choo shoes, or tail-slam her belongings.

"This isn't working for me, babe," said Anthony one Saturday afternoon after they spent another day with Goober in the dog park. "This is getting boring. We can't go out on weekends, we're always staying in . . . I can't see my friends. I mean, we can't spend time with our friends," he quickly corrected.

"Not only boring," added Jennifer, "it's stressful. I'm always watching Goober to be sure he doesn't think one of my fur-lined coats is another dog he can hump. My landlord sent me a warning letter stating that people are complaining about the dog –sticking his snout in crotches, or slobbering on their shoes. The letter demanded that the dog has to go, or I'll be evicted for violating my lease. Anthony, you've got to take Goober back to your parents' house, and stay there with him."

After a few moments, Anthony suggested, "Babe, I've been thinking. Maybe, we should buy a house together."

Jennifer paused. "Is that a marriage proposal, Anthony? I'm not going to buy a house with someone I'm dating."

"Hey babe. You know I love you. Why do we need a piece of paper to prove it? Let's do all the things married people do, like buy a house, fix it up, and get some furniture. We already have a dog. We're a couple, right? Don't you think it's time we thought about buying a place together?"

"*You* have a dog, Anthony," Jennifer said. "*I'm* the one who takes care of him. So, is this a marriage proposal, Anthony?" She was relentless.

"Sure, if you want." Anthony calculated his next move. He had to be careful not to get himself into a commitment he'd regret. He guessed he loved Jennifer, but it was her money he loved more.

"I want to keep my apartment . . . just in case," she said snapping him out of his reverie.

"Absolutely, babe. Besides, all your shoes wouldn't fit into any house we buy together," he said with a chuckle. "We can plan a wedding. Maybe, for next year."

And, Jennifer believed him.

The following Sunday, they went to the dog park, and while Goober chased squirrels, Anthony looked through the real estate section.

"How much money do you have to put towards a down payment?" he asked her.

She hesitated for a moment before answering, "I'm not really sure."

Anthony's mind raced, *Could it be she doesn't have the money I think she has?*

Finally, Jennifer said, "I've got at least $75,000 we can put towards the down payment. I received a $375,000 buyout from Simone, but that money is being invested for my future. I really can't touch that. I might be able to scrape up another $10,000, but we'll need money for closing costs."

Jennifer turned and noted Anthony's shocked face. "What's wrong?"

"Nothing. I didn't think you had that sort of money," he lied. What he actually thought was: *What the hell did you do with all the money you made working? Buying shoes, clothes, and other shit is going to stop after we buy a house.*

"Can you match that?" she asked.

"Sure," he answered, but he knew he didn't have anywhere near that amount of money. He'd have to ask his parents for a loan.

Jennifer and Anthony loved being by the beach, so they concentrated their search from Devon up to Woodmont in Milford. They settled on a modest three bedroom, two bath house in the Point Beach area, yards from the water. The house sat like a huge bird's nest, twenty feet high on cement stilts, featuring the latest technology systems to protect it against a major hurricane.

Committing to being co-owners of a house was a big step for Jennifer. She had always rented, saying she didn't want the responsibilities involved in home maintenance. She believed Anthony when he said it wasn't a lot of work when two people shared the load, but sharing the responsibilities, according to Anthony, seemed to be one sided – Jennifer's side.

"What assurance do I have, Anthony that we'll get married? I don't want to be working at my job forever. Don't you want to start a family in the next year or so?"

Anthony blurted out, "Wow, that's a lot to take in, babe." A bead of sweat formed across his upper lip. "Let's get settled in the house, and then we'll start planning a wedding."

And so they moved in. Anthony avoided the subject of marriage for months. When Jennifer began pushing him to put together a guest list, and visit wedding venues, he resisted again, and their conversations turned into heated fights. Jennifer wanted to get married and start a family. Anthony wanted to live the life of a bachelor, yet, have the security of a woman at home to satisfy his wants and needs.

One night after dinner, Jennifer tried bringing up the subject of a wedding venue, again, and could they start their search?

"I've been thinking about that, babe," he lied. "How about we have a small wedding in my parents' backyard? It'll save us a lot of money."

"That's fine. Home weddings can be delightful, but there are a lot of problems, too."

"Like what?" he asked.

"Well, let's say we have a small wedding of 50 people. Then again, that's your immediate family," she joked. "We'll have more like 75 people. That's a lot of bathroom flushing. And if we have a caterer, that's more water going down into your parents' septic system. We'd have to rent tables, chairs, china, glasses, flatware, and all the rest. We'll need a tent. And have a Plan B."

"Plan B? What's that?" Anthony asked, already thinking this was way more than he could handle.

Jennifer explained, "If it rains, or there's a major storm, we can't have the reception in your parents' backyard. Even if we had a tent, it might not work. So, we have to adjust and have the reception inside the house. Sometimes a home wedding is more work than having it in a restaurant."

She reflected, "Simone and I did several home weddings. Most were beautiful and successful. And I'm sure we won't have to worry about this with your family, but Simone always hired an undercover cop for home weddings."

"What?" Anthony shouted. "I ain't having no cops at my wedding."

"Calm down. No one would know he or she was a cop. We'll say they're a relative on my side of the family."

"I don't like it. Why would you want a cop, anyway?"

"Because people steal, that's why. We've placed discrete cameras throughout homes, and have caught people doing some very weird things. Our undercover cop found a guest rummaging through the owner's master bedroom dresser. One guest stole pills from inside a locked closet. They knew the wife was on pain meds, and they prowled until they found the prescription pills. Once, we saw a relative trying to open a safe inside his cousin's closet. At another wedding, we saw a teenage couple having sex on the bed."

Anthony stared in shock.

"I know, Anthony. Everyone says 'not my family' but the reality is, people steal, they snoop, and they take advantage of the homeowners.

If we're going to have a wedding at your parents' home, I'm hiring an undercover policeman. And you'll never know who the person is. Anthony, you wouldn't believe some of the experiences Simone and I had over our years together." The words stuck in her throat, nostalgia taking over. She cleared her throat, and said, "Okay, back to us. When do you want to set a date? And do you still want to have it at your parents' house?"

"Oh," Anthony said, his mind racing. He remained quiet and finally said, "I know my mother. She'd want us to get married at the house. All of my sisters had big weddings in banquet halls. She said that when Vinny or me gets married, she wants us to have the wedding at the house," he lied.

"Okay, just as long as your parents understand there is a lot involved in a home wedding." Jennifer took in a deep breath and waited before asking, "When?"

"When, what?" he asked, fully knowing what she was asking.

"A date, Anthony! I'm asking you for a wedding date to set for our wedding." She was fed up from his game playing.

Jennifer was married two other times. The first time, she was drunk, and the marriage lasted until the next morning, then annulled. The second time, she thought she knew the guy, but he overdosed on oxycodone, and died eight days later. She hoped that marriage number three wasn't a complete strike-out.

Why was this so difficult? In her mind, the other marriages didn't count. This time was different. She had a real connection to Anthony, and she knew if he grew up a little, they'd be the perfect couple.

"Well? When are you thinking?" she repeated.

"I know my dad wants to put on a new roof and siding. Maybe after those projects are done. And Theresa's kid is receiving Holy Communion next year. Maybe after that?"

"Anthony," she responded, "I think you're buying time again."

"That's not true."

"What assurance do I have that we'll get married in the next year?" She began wondering why she was pushing the issue.

"I love you, babe, and we'll get married one day. We need to save up money again. This house cost a lot more than we thought."

Anthony paused before continuing, "How about I make you my beneficiary on my life insurance policy? Would that convince you?"

"I guess," Jennifer said, hesitantly. She thought discussing life insurance was a strange subject to bring up at that moment. "Simone and I would discuss this with engaged couples, especially if one person was married before and never changed their beneficiary. Or, if they had a prenuptial agreement, or a large estate where assets or children were involved."

"Yeah, so?" he asked, not paying attention to what she was saying, or where she was going with the discussion. His mind was still processing the undercover cop stories.

"One of the most important things we did when working with couples, was to approach subjects the engaged couple never thought about before getting married."

"Are you going to start on that, again?" he asked, annoyed.

"Yes, the Triple D's," Jennifer said. "Discuss. Decide. Document."

"I think it means big tits," Anthony guffawed.

"Anthony!" snapped Jennifer. "Stop it, and listen to what I'm saying," her annoyance was escalating. "Couples, like us need to discuss several subjects, like children, money, religion, or where we are spending the holidays. When we come to a decision, we'll document what we've agreed to."

"There's nothing to discuss, babe. I'm the man of the house, and I'll make all the decisions."

"I hope you're joking, Anthony."

"Of course I am, babe," he smirked. "Tell me what you want to talk about. There can't be that much."

"Actually, there is a lot to discuss. For example, meals. Who will do the cooking?"

"You," said Anthony. "I don't know how to cook, and I have no interest in learning. None whatsoever. If you don't want to cook, I'll go to my mom's. Next subject," he said cutting Jennifer off before she had a comeback.

Jennifer stalled for a moment, then said, "Religion. I don't practice any religion. I've not seen you go to church on Sundays, but if we have kids, do you want to raise them with a religion?"

"We can figure that out when we have kids. I can't decide that now."

Jennifer was on a roll, and couldn't stop asking what she considered were relevant questions. "What about Christmas? I usually go to my mom's in Long Island. She's alone, so I make it a point to spend time with her. I . . ."

"Babe," Anthony said cutting her off, "there's no way I'm going out to Long Island for Christmas. No way," he emphasized. "Your mom can come here, or you can go there. But don't expect me to deal with holiday traffic. Besides, Christmas morning is a big deal in the Palmieri household. All the kids come to our house the night before. My mom makes the traditional seven-fishes for dinner, everybody sleeps over . . . on the floor, sofa, everywhere. Then on Christmas morning, we open presents. I ain't missing that to go to your mother's house."

"What about Carmine's family?"

"What about them? They ain't welcomed to our house no more. Carmine stole money from my grandfather. Everybody in the family knows that. I don't know what they do for Christmas, and I don't care. Christmas will be at my parents' house, starting on Christmas Eve."

"But Anthony," Jennifer started to say, but got cut off again.

"Nope. I ain't discussing this. Decision made. Christmas is at my family's house. You can document that," he said in a snarky tone. "Next subject."

Jennifer had a bad feeling about how this discussion was moving – actually, <u>not</u> moving.

"Kids."

"Yeah, I want kids. Lots of them. But I ain't changing diapers, or taking them to the park, or doing homework. That's your job."

"My job?" asked Jennifer. "Which brings me to the next subject: am I going to stay home with the kids, or will you expect me to continue working?"

"My mom can take care of the kids. You can work," he said, already knowing the answers to all of Jennifer's questions. "Hey babe, this is easy. What else you going to ask me?"

Jennifer's stomach churned. She inhaled, realizing Anthony wasn't ready for these questions. Maybe he'd never be. Simone and she always pushed couples to discuss these subjects before getting married. It was important. They discovered many times couples were planning a wedding, and not a marriage.

She faced her next question, "Why do you want to marry me?"

"Babe, you're getting mushy on me," Anthony said taking her in his arms. "I love you. I want you to be my wife. We're soul mates, remember? When we first met, you felt it, too."

Jennifer had to admit, those were the words she used describing Anthony to Simone. But she also remembered Barbara Kemp who thought her fiancé, Biff would change after they were married. She recalled the results of his bad behavior.

Jennifer's thoughts were deflected by Anthony. "Let's talk about these things another day. Right now, I think it's time we locked Goober out of the bedroom."

Ten

At Francine's weekly Canasta game with Patty, Rhoda, and Marie, she'd regularly complain about Jennifer, simply because Jennifer wasn't a "nice, Italian girl," like Angie, her son Vinny's girlfriend.

Francine bragged, "Angie can make a braciole that would make an Iron Chef cry. Her gravy is divine, and her meatballs soft like pillows."

"Why don't you like Jennifer? Doesn't she cook?" Marie asked.

"Cook? All she cooks is beef stew in a crock pot. It drives Anthony's dog crazy smelling the food all day. The other thing she knows how to make is reservations. I'm telling you, my Anthony needs to meet a nice Italian girl. This one needs lessons on how to take care of her man. She won't listen to me."

Marie asked, "Why does he stay with her if she can't cook?

"I think she has a golden mouth," Anthony's mother responded while contemplating the cards in her hand.

"Francine! Don't say that," snapped her partner, Patty.

"Eww!" responded the other women.

"Don't talk about Jennifer that way. She seems like a nice girl . . . always dresses pretty. I wish I could wear heels like that, but at my age, my bunions would have me arrested," said Marie.

"She's taller than my Anthony in those things," Francine said. "That's not right. A girl should be shorter than her boyfriend."

"That's nonsense," Patty retorted. "Now, are you going to throw out a card, or do you want to sit around and gossip about your twins all day?"

"When is your other son going to make an honest woman of Angie?" inquired Rhoda. "They've been going out for years."

"Yeah, since high school. My Vinny ain't ready to settle down."

"Does Angie know Vinny has a goomada?" Marie asked.

Francine paused, looked up, and locked eyes with her opponent, "Why are you being such a bitch?"

Marie straighten up in her chair, pushed back her shoulders and snapped, "You know it's true, Francine. Why are you always protecting him?"

"I don't want to talk about it," Francine said, throwing down a duce on the pile of cards.

"Are you sure you want to put down that card?" asked her partner, Patty.

"Shit," Francine yelped as she attempted to grab the card back.

But Rhoda put her hand on top of Francine's, stopping her from taking back a jewel of a card.

"Flustered by the truth, Franny?" Marie said, escalating the tension. She knew that calling her "Franny" would add fuel to the fire.

"It's your fault I put down that card," said Francine looking at Marie, her anger and voice increasing.

"Ladies," announced Patty, "let's end this conversation and concentrate on the game."

"She started it," Francine said pointing a finger at Marie.

Marie fueled the situation by adding, "You just can't face the truth about Vinny and Angie. He's with her because *you* like her. Because she would make him a good Italian wife. You don't like Jennifer because she's not Italian and can't cook a Sunday dinner like Angie. Meanwhile, Anthony seems faithful to her and not cat-calling around town like his brother. You're angry that your boys won't get married and give you more grandchildren."

"Enough!" Francine shouted. "I'm done with this game." She slammed her cards down, and stood to leave.

"Sit down Francine," Patty said, her voice raised. "You two can take this outside after the game. Not now, and not in my house. Francine and Marie, you two are acting like schoolgirls. Francine, pick up your cards and let's finish this game."

Francine paused, then followed Patty's orders. She sat down, picked up her cards, and refocused on her hand.

The tension lingered, thick with anger and jealousy. Francine knew Marie was right. She headed home after the game, waving off lunch at the diner, where the foursome went every week.

"I'm getting one of my headaches," Francine feigned. "I'll see you all next week at my house."

As Francine drove home after the Canasta game, she recounted the times that she had turned a blind eye to her boys' antics. Once, she witnessed a woman sneaking out of the basement at five forty-five a.m. Francine had gotten up early, awakened by the birds singing outside her bedroom window. Vinny assumed his mother was still asleep. Instead, Francine was sitting at the kitchen table drinking a cup of coffee when she heard the Bilco doors open. Her son, dressed only in boxer shorts, emerged from the basement, followed by a woman scantily dressed. The basement was Vinny's domain, except when the grandkids came to play. He had his own bedroom, which he kept locked, a bathroom and a small kitchen. Francine cooked and cleaned for him as well, but never saw signs of another woman, until that morning. She thought the evidence of sexual activity had been between Vinny and Angie.

While her son and the mystery woman kissed, Vinny ran his hands over her body, and she, his.

Francine dumped the rest of her coffee into the sink, and quickly ran upstairs to her bedroom, fearing Vinny would come into the kitchen looking for something to drink, or eat. She laid down on her bed, her heart pounding, anger and shame coursing through her.

An hour later she heard Vinny clanking dishes in the kitchen. Francine returned and brewed a fresh cup of coffee. They sat at the table, and while he ate a bowl of cold cereal and she a large piece of pound cake, they discussed his upcoming day. Afterwards, he picked up his laptop carrying bag and placed the strap on his shoulder. As he was about to leave, she said, "Vincent Michael."

He stopped short. His given name was never said, unless he was in trouble. Francine said his name in a soft tone which spoke volumes. He turned and faced his mother.

"Yeah, ma?"

"Don't bring that puttana to my house no more."

Feigning innocence, as if his mother was a stupid woman, he said, "Who, ma? Angie?"

"You know who I'm talking about. I saw her. No more. Capese?"

Vinny didn't respond. No words, no acknowledgement meant no guilt in the Palmieri Family.

He opened the door and left for work. Francine sat at the table and wiped away tears. She reflected on how she had pushed Vinny to invite Angie to Sunday dinner. She had welcomed Angie into her home like another daughter. Her intent was to push him into a more committed relationship. Why? Because Angie was a nice Italian girl, whom she liked to have as a daughter-in-law, with no regard for her son's feelings towards her. What Marie had said that day, was true – he did have a goomada, and I only like Angie because she's Italian.

Her eyes moved to the counter where Vinny's brown bag lunch sat. She scooped it up, and ran to the front door.

Meanwhile, Vinny was angry at himself that his mother caught him with Joanie - mad for not being able to afford to live with Anthony, or have his own place. *Anthony has the perfect set up*, he thought. *Mom cooks and cleans for him, and he has Jennifer for everything else. Yeah, Jennifer's a sap, but he doesn't have his mommy scolding him for bringing home a woman.*

He couldn't do to Angie what Ant does to Jennifer. Angie would jump at the chance to live with him. She longed for an engagement ring on her finger, and a firm wedding date before she'd agree to live together.

She saw how Jennifer was itching for a marriage proposal. She wasn't willing to give up her independence only to be a live-in girlfriend.

Vinny pondered, *I'm going to have to stop seeing Joanie. I wonder how long mom knew about her coming over.*

Vinny went outside, put his work bag and coffee cup on the roof of the car, and hung up his jacket in the back seat. He slammed the back door, grabbed his case and coffee from the roof of the car. Just as he was about to get into the front seat, he heard his mother's call.

"Vinny, you forgot your lunch."

He walked over to her, said a timid thank you, got back into his car, and drove away.

Francine went back inside the house, and began watching the shows she recorded the previous night. Her mind wandered to Anthony. She suspected he, too, had been seeing his former girlfriend, Fran, behind Jennifer's back. She hated Fran -- the girl that shared her name. She didn't dislike her -- she hated her.

Anthony had once brought her home for Sunday dinner. Unfortunately, the woman didn't have any fashion sense, or didn't own any decent clothes. She dressed too provocatively for his family's taste. Well, maybe by his mother's standards, but Vinny and his father enjoyed the expansive cleavage she proudly displayed. Instantly, Francine took a dislike to her, not only because of her name, but because of her lack of respect by dressing like a hooker.

After too many glasses of wine for a respectable lady, Francine asked the big question: "So Fran, what do you do for a living?"

"I work at the *The Cat's Meow*," she answered without filtering her reply.

"That a strip club," Anthony's father announced. His wife gave him a look that implied, *And you know this how?*

"And what do you do there?" asked Francine.

"I'm a pole dancer," Fran answered, suddenly realizing Anthony hadn't told his family of her occupation.

"I see," mumbled his father. He looked at his wife and said in Italian, "Don't say anything. We'll talk about this later."

They ate in silence for the rest of the meal. Coffee and dessert weren't offered, and it became apparent the meal was over once the dishes were cleared from the table.

After a forced, "Thank you for a lovely meal," Anthony took Fran back to her apartment.

"I think I need to go back home. I shouldn't stay tonight," Anthony announced at Fran's door. "I don't think my parents were happy about your job. I should have warned you that they're old fashioned. Knowing my parents, I think it best we don't see each other again in public." Anthony stammered, stared at his shoes, and admitted, "Look, I'm sort of seeing someone else," he said. "She's going to be moving in full time in a few weeks." Then he looked up at Fran and added, "Well . . . maybe you and I can see each other without anyone else knowing."

Fran wasn't surprised. She knew her occupation caused pre-determined opinions. But she needed to work nights so she could go to school during the day, and be able to pay her rent. This wasn't the first time she'd heard a guy announce he was married, or living with someone, or that she wasn't accepted by his family.

"I understand," she whispered. "Call me when you can," closing the door behind her.

Back home, Anthony got an earful from his mother.

"I knew it. She's a puttana, Anthony," his mother screamed at him. "She's not to step foot into this house again. Do you understand me?"

"But ma, she's really a very nice girl," Anthony said defensively. "Once you know her, you'll see what I mean."

"Is there anything more to see?" his father said. "She left very little to the imagination."

Receiving a warning look from his wife, Johnny continued, "I agree with your mother, Anthony, she's not to come here again. And I'd advise you not to see her any longer. Who knows what diseases she's got in that 'peesh'," his father said.

"Pop," Anthony snapped. "She's not that kind of girl," he said unconvincingly.

Everyone in that room knew what kind of girl she was, short of wearing a neon sign on her chest. She wasn't welcomed in the Palmieri Family circle, period. Anthony acquiesced to his parents' demands and never brought Fran back to their home. But that didn't stop him from seeing her, whenever he was able to get away from Jennifer.

Boys will be boys, Francine decided. That's what the Palmieri men do, she tried to convince herself. Or did they?

Eleven

Simone Simpson stared out into space, her mind wondered aimlessly. A phone rang in the distance.

"Simone, it's for you," announced Katy, snapping Simone out of her reverie. "It's Judy Smith."

She picked up the office phone, wondering why Judy was calling on the office line, and not her personal cell phone.

"Hi Judy. Is everything okay?"

"Everything is fine, but I've been trying to reach you all day. It's not like you not to respond to a call or text. Is your phone shut off?"

Simone grabbed her cell from the bottom of her purse, and saw she had missed four calls, had three voicemail messages, and nine text messages. "Oh, my goodness, Judy. I shut off my phone at the Chamber meeting this morning, and forgot to turn it back on. Is everything okay?"

"Everything is perfect," Judy said. "Harold and I have set a date, and we want you to be our maid of honor."

Teasing her best friend, she responded, "And not your wedding planner?"

"Not this time, Simone," Judy said chuckling. "If Harold and I don't work out, you'll be the first planner I'll call for marriage number two," she teased.

The women met at New York University, where they were roommates, and quickly became best friends. Judy's parents became Simone's adopted parents after Simone's father abandoned her for leaving Louisville, and for making a life of her own. Jean-Paul, Simone's brother, who still lived in Louisville with his wife and children, also cut off all communication with her. After Simone's parents died, as a result of her father driving drunk, Virginia, Henry and Judy Smith became Simone's only family. After Mr. Smith's death, he bequeathed to Simone a penthouse apartment in Paris. His daughter Judy inherited a similar apartment across the hall.

"So, tell me, Simone, how does it feel to be married?"

"Judy, I couldn't be happier," Simone said. "I find myself hoping it's not a dream. It took me a long time to get over Joe's sudden death, and my fear of losing Charlie surfaces every once in a while. He's very patient. We talk about my fears ad nauseam."

She continued, "Losing Jennifer as a friend and business partner has had a major impact on my life. I know, now, that her leaving the business at the time was the right thing to do. Maybe not a complete cut off – we should have made more of an effort to work things out. No, I should have made more of an effort. I miss her ability to make me laugh no matter how dire the situation. I miss her spunk, and her ability to know what I'm thinking without a word passing between us. As my attorney, Sid once said, 'She's the yin to your yang.' And he was so right."

"Well, maybe she'll come back to the company," Judy said, trying to console her friend.

"I doubt she would consider returning. I think her pride is too great to admit she made some terrible decisions during her last months with the company."

"Do you know what she's doing now?"

"I've no clue. She's probably married to Anthony, and has a bunch of kids by now. I've sent her emails, texts and a few phone messages, but she never answered."

"Well, from this moment on, all you have to do is concentrate on being my maid of honor," Judy said, moving Simone's focus from

Jennifer to herself. "We've set next May nineteenth as our date. I want to get married at the house, Simone. The blossoms at that time of year are magnificent. It'll be a small gathering, approximately thirty to thirty-five people. Harold's parents, his brother who will be the best man, and one aunt. And our friends."

Judy added, "Oh, Simone, I'm so excited. Maybe you'll consider moving your company to Richmond so that we can live closer. I'm sure Charlie can take over management of a large hotel down south."

"You're dreaming, my friend. Charlie and I are beach folks. Besides, "I Do" has become a major event and wedding planning company in Connecticut. I'd have to start all over down south. Why don't you and Harold consider getting teaching jobs up north?"

"Not with my mom still living in Charlottesville. I could never leave her alone," Judy said somberly. "She's only in her early sixties, but since my dad died, she's aged. I know she'd never move from the family home. Fortunately, she has Irene to watch over her . . . cook, clean, take her to doctor's appointments."

"Has she been ill?"

"She's slowed down. She spends her days sitting on the porch, rocking away, daydreaming. I'm sure she's thinking of my dad, and reliving their lives together. She fell two weeks ago. She didn't break anything, but another fall could result in broken bones."

The two women talked about Judy's plans for her wedding for twenty minutes.

Simone looked at the clock and said, "Judy, I hate to cut you short, but I've got several text messages to answer, and phone calls to return. We've got a very large wedding coming up this weekend, and I've got a lot of i's to dot, and t's to cross."

"Thanks for your wedding suggestions, Simone. I'll discuss them with Harold this evening."

"Let's catch up soon," the women said simultaneously, followed by a laugh.

Twelve

"I Do" LLC continued to thrive, overcoming upheavals which usually only happened on reality TV. Last year, Simone was distracted with her own life dramas. She had been receiving text messages from a burner phone, supposedly sent from her deceased husband, Joe. Someone was entering her home while she was out: her underwear was stolen, followed by dozens of roses being left on her kitchen counter, and someone planted a camera in her bedside lampshade. Added to the stress, her boyfriend, Charlie was going through an agonizing divorce, and Simone's adopted father, Mr. Smith, died.

On the night of an office holiday party that Simone was hosting at her home, the person who had been entering her home and sending text messages from her deceased husband, revealed himself. He had professed his love for her, and his need to possess her. Violence ensued, and Simone was forced to defend her life.

Hours later, while she and Jennifer were in the hospital attending to Charlie, whom the perpetrator had attempted to kill hours earlier, Jennifer revealed to Simone that she had suspected this person for months. Jennifer knew about the text messages being sent to Simone, and the invasions in her home. If Jennifer had immediately shared this information with Simone, the evening's events might have been stopped, before the violence escalated. Tragedies might have been averted. Jennifer admitted she'd had Anthony's father's friend do surveillance on this suspect. The results showed this person wasn't who he said he was. Jennifer never revealed this because she wanted to get even with Simone for dismissing Anthony as her soul mate.

Simone walked away from her friend and partner vowing never to speak or see her again until they sat in an attorney's office, officially documenting the end of their relationship.

Jennifer's removal put a strain on the office dynamics. Simone had lost a trusted and hard-working friend and partner in Jennifer. And, if it hadn't been for the quick thinking by the Greenwich Police, Charlie would have been lost as well.

Simone received a letter from Jennifer's attorney requesting a buyout of her share of the company. The letter was like a death notice to Simone. She had foolishly thought that once Jennifer had time to calm down and consider her mistakes, her partner would come back to the business.

She had phoned Jennifer several times, but her calls landed on deaf ears. As a result, future communication between the two women was solely through their attorneys. Simone suspected the break was fueled by Anthony, and just another impulsive action by Jennifer. Until Jennifer realized that many of her life decisions were made without much thoughtful consideration, she would continue to live her life making serious mistakes and hurting others along the way.

The next time Simone saw her business partner, four months had passed. They sat across from each other in the attorney's office. There, they signed documents to sever their relationship forever.

Once the papers were signed, Jennifer would be released from any future holdings as a partner in "I Do" LLC. She would be restricted from contacting any previous or existing clients of the said company for a two-year period, and from opening her own event planning company within a one-hundred mile radius of the Town of Fairfield.

"One-hundred miles," shouted Jennifer. "That's ridiculous. I can agree, and understand being restricted to Fairfield County, but one-hundred miles includes New York and New Jersey – that's extortion."

"Precisely," Jennifer's attorney told her.

Sidney Harding, Simone's attorney interrupted. "Your reputation in the tristate area precedes you, Ms. Keys. In order to protect my client's interest, we must demand these restrictions."

Simone watched red blotches slowly appear on Jennifer's chest and gradually creep up to her hair line. Simone knew the signs and the symptoms all too well - Jennifer was about to cry. Surprisingly, her soon-to-be ex-partner kept her emotions in check, and avoided eye contact with Simone.

After conferring with her incompetent and inexperienced attorney, Jennifer agreed to the terms. In the back of her mind, she schemed to open her own business one-hundred and one miles from Fairfield. *That'll fix her,* she thought. But Jennifer did not read the extra-fine print in the agreement, which stated she was also restricted from doing business in a one-hundred mile radius. She could open an office one-hundred and one miles away, but could not contract with anyone in that same radius. She would have to move several states away in order to satisfy those demands.

At the end of the contract signing, Jennifer received a check from Simone Simpson for $375,000 as payoff to finalize her partnership in the company. Over the years, Simone made that amount several times over; quite often working just a few large weddings. The payout was, in her mind, a small amount to sacrifice to get Jennifer out of her office and out of her life, no matter how painful the loss.

Jennifer's attorney handed his client the check. Jennifer placed it in her pocketbook, stood up, and walked out of the room. No goodbyes, no handshakes, no salutations. The payoff was good, but all the money in the world would not bring back the friendship she and Simone had once shared.

Several months had now passed since Jennifer Keys left "I Do". Simone found the void profoundly difficult, and she found herself missing Jennifer, despite all the repercussions that had ensued.

Thirteen

Years ago, after Simone was seriously injured by the speeding taxi that killed her husband and unborn child, she needed to begin a new life. She sold her condo in Tribeca and moved to the Smith's home in Charlottesville, North Carolina. Here she stayed and recharged for over two years. Finally, she convinced her best friend, Judy Smith to go with her to an event-planner's conference in Washington, DC. Here, Simone met Jennifer Keys and the two instantly became friends and colleagues. Simone was often hired as an independent contractor, working side by side with Jennifer on high-end weddings, mostly at New York City venues. When the proprietor decided to sell the business and move to Florida, Jennifer called Simone, thinking she'd be interested in purchasing the company.

Katy Lewiston, Jonathan Vasquez, and Jennifer Keys had worked for the previous owner of the company. When Simone agreed to purchase the company, she offered Jennifer 10% ownership of the newly named company, "I Do" LLC. Shortly after, the two women created an eclectic, energetic and professional company, with weddings booked two and three years in advance, with budgets starting at $250,000 to over $4 million.

Simone moved from the Smith home and purchased an old beach cottage on Compo Road in Westport, across from the beach. She worked closely with Pete Cody, a contractor, and with an interior designer, overseeing the inner and outer changes to the structure. Together they created a spectacular home.

Presently, the events planning side of the business – birthday parties, specialty events, and corporate functions – were being spearheaded by Katy Lewiston. After Simone purchased the business, Katy worked as a part-time planner, organizing Sweet Sixteen parties, baby showers, and other children's events. Once her son left for college, and she and her husband became empty-nesters, Katy had more available time to dedicate to the business. Over the last year, she developed into a professional and detail-oriented anchor of "I Do".

Wedding season was fast approaching, and Simone's work load was mounting. Although Katy and some of the other temps were capable, no one since Jennifer had the knowledge of handling the stresses involved with high-end weddings. She knew she didn't have many options . . . she needed to hire another professional planner, or two, and soon.

She employed Cindy Hom, a Certified Festival and Events Executive (CFEE), and a Professional Wedding Planner designated by the Association of Bridal Consultants (ABC). She had lived in the Park Slope area of Brooklyn before moving to Shelton, Connecticut less than twenty minutes from the office. She had nine years' experience in the business, specializing in Chinese weddings. Her résumé was very impressive, and after a short interview, Simone hired her on a probationary period of one year. Termination, if warranted, could be at any time.

One morning, Cindy danced her way into Simone's office, surprising her boss by the routine. Cindy wore teal colored yoga pants, and a black tank top that barely touched the waistband of her pants. Her thick long black hair was tied in a ponytail that swayed side to side with her movements.

"Simone, maybe I should put on my business card: I specialize in ABC/WASP weddings."

The suggestion fell flat. "I don't get it," said Simone, sincerely.

Cindy explained, "ABC stands for American Born Chinese, and WASP is White Anglo-Saxon Protestant. I specialize in inter-racial weddings," Cindy said with forced enthusiasm, awaiting a laugh from her boss.

Trying to keep her reaction under control, Simone responded, "I don't think that's appropriate. I thought ABC stood for Association of

Bridal Consultants. If you're going to use those letters, also use CFEE. Cindy, I'd prefer you not say ABC relates to your nationality."

Cindy stared at Simone, turned, and left her boss's office. "Grump," Cindy mumbled under her breath.

Simone began questioning her decision to hire Cindy. She had good credentials, but her sense of humor, and her immaturity left a lot to be desired. She'd often come to work in tight pants, leaving very little to the imagination, or jeans torn at the knees, and skimpy tank tops. Simone never implemented rules, but she assumed that a woman with an education in business would know, and understand, the professional dress code. Life was more casual in beach towns, and people 'dressed down' but this was going too far.

Simone's goal was to expand her business to include more cultural diversification, starting with Cindy. And, she had increased the business by 7% over six months, working largely Chinese-American weddings. Once news got out that "I Do" had a specialist in this area, referrals grew as a direct result of Cindy.

Although "I Do" prospered, its reputation sturdy and the income increasing, Simone still felt something was missing. The empty spot was Jennifer Keys. Simone didn't have the same enthusiasm without her friend and partner. She vowed to make more of an effort to reach out to Jennifer, and try to make amends.

One month after Cindy joined "I Do", Simone hired Gary Garrison "GG" who lived in Westport. He was a skilled venue designer, and quickly became a great asset to her company. Often, Simone had to hire independent interior venue designers who created custom-painted backdrops, flooring, lighting designs, and built structures to match the event's theme. They worked closely with the florist, and often, were very successful producing the flawless atmosphere for the special day.

Unfortunately, GG and Cindy were like oil and water, often disagreeing on layout and design ideas, with Simone being the peacemaker. She was certain, and hopeful, that after a few months of working together, they'd iron out their differences, but the future looked bleak.

Otherwise, one of them would have to go, a decision she didn't want to consider.

Simone knew Jennifer would be able to corral GG and Cindy. She and Jennifer worked well together for seven years, five of those years Jennifer was Simone's business partner, confidant, and friend. Cindy and GG were terrific, but they lacked the spirit and humor Jennifer provided.

At the time of their split, Jennifer was dating Anthony Palmieri. For some reason, mostly instinctual, Simone took an immediate dislike to him even before she met him. Some of what Jennifer confided to Simone about their relationship, caused Simone's inner alarms to sound. Jennifer was impulsive, and often hooked up with inappropriate men. Jennifer had two unsuccessful marriages. Simone might have pre-judged Anthony, but knowing Jennifer's personality and impetuous nature, she feared her friend was getting involved with another manipulative man. After weeks of dating Anthony, Jennifer moved in with him.

At Jennifer's father's funeral, her mother asked Simone to watch over her daughter. She was concerned that Jennifer chased after the wrong men, and one day she'd meet up with the devil himself.

Simone drove past Jennifer's apartment in Fairfield several times, but the lights were off and the shades drawn. She speculated Jennifer had moved into Anthony's beach cottage, after all. They never ran into each other at other events, and venue managers had said they hadn't seen or heard about her whereabouts.

Was it possible Jennifer was married and had kids by now? Simone smiled at the thought of a pregnant Jennifer wearing her signature six-inch spike heels. She'd probably wear them during delivery.

Suddenly, Simone's cell phone rang, snapping her back to reality.

"Hello."

"How's my bride this morning?"

"I'm having an unproductive morning . . . and you?"

"The same," Charlie answered. "Is everything okay? You seemed distracted this morning, so I wanted to see how you're feeling."

Simone closed her office door, and lowered her voice. "I'm good, but I am having second thoughts about Cindy. I'm not sure she's the right fit for our team."

"You had mentioned your concerns to me weeks ago. I thought you two had discussed office protocol."

"I did. But she seems to be set in her ways," Simone said. "Charlie, I really can't talk about it now, maybe this evening."

"Of course, my love."

"Some good news, though," she added. "I spoke to Judy. She and Gordon have set a wedding date for next year. I'm so excited for her."

"That's wonderful news," said Charlie. "I'm sure Mrs. Smith is thrilled. Gordon seems like a nice, respectful southern gentleman."

"That's a perfect description of him – a southern gentleman." Switching subjects, she said, "Charlie, I've been thinking a lot about Jennifer. She drove me crazy sometimes, but she also made me smile, even when things appeared bleak. And she was a one-of-a-kind wedding planner. I just hope she's okay, and nothing has happened to her. My gut is telling me she's in trouble."

"I'm sure she's fine, Simone. Have you tried calling her, maybe she's afraid to call you, thinking you're still angry over what happened?"

"I've tried, but the calls go to voicemail. And she never returns any of them."

"I know how to make you smile, my love," Charlie responded teasingly.

"Don't make me blush. My employees can see me in this fishbowl."

The two lovers continued their intimate banter. Simone looked at her watch, and said, "Charlie, I'd love to continue this conversation, but I have to get some work done. Can we go to DaPietro's tonight? I need to twirl spaghetti to calm my anxiety."

"Absolutely. You know, Simone, if Pietro wasn't married, I'd be a little jealous at how he makes you swoon over his food."

Simone laughed loudly, causing Katy to take an inquiring look.

"Thanks for the chuckle, Charlie. I needed that. I've got research to do. Cindy and I are going to Manhattan tomorrow to consult with a client. I need to become educated on a formal, traditional Chinese wedding. See you tonight. I love you."

"I love you too, my wife."

'My wife.' The words softened her heart. Yes, she was married to Charles Hamilton VI. After the death of her first husband, she didn't believe she'd ever love again, but Charlie's patience and love proved her wrong. Their relationship started years ago as a one-night passionate fling. At the time, Simone refused to let her feelings for Charlie consume her. He was going through a divorce, and she had enough drama from her staff and clients to allow herself to become more involved. He was never far from her mind, just like this moment. She smiled.

Suddenly, her thoughts turned to Jennifer. Her stomach lurched. *Something's not right,* she mused. *No, something's not right.*

Fourteen

The next day, Simone and Cindy were scheduled to meet the Lee family in Chinatown on the Lower East Side. The couple had asked to meet Simone before agreeing to hire her. They knew Cindy and her family for many years, but wanted to be sure their friend's daughter was working for a reputable and honest woman. "You can tell trust by a person's eyes," they told Cindy.

Admittedly, Simone was apprehensive as to what Cindy would wear for the meeting. She met Simone at the Westport Train Station wearing a gray pencil skirt that landed just below her knees, a long sleeve white blouse, a strand of pearls, a pair of gray one-inch heels, and a Louis Vuitton pocketbook. *Very conservative,* Simone thought. *Maybe there's hope.*

The women rode the train to Grand Central Terminal, then boarded the 6 Train to Canal Street. From there they walked to Pell Street. They entered the 1800s tenement building, and walked up three flights. Aromas of foods from different lands filled the hallways, along with the sounds of children's laughter. Cindy knocked on the wooden door, and they faced an elderly couple in their late eighties. Both had faces with deep-set lines that were maps of their lives -- their struggles, happiness, and years of hard work.

"Simone Simpson, meet Mr. and Mrs. Lee." The couple bowed to Simone, and she returned the greeting.

Mrs. Lee spoke to Cindy in Chinese, while she waved her hand and invited them into her clean and modest apartment. Simone had no idea what they were saying, but there was lots of smiles and bowing. More foreign language was spoken, some directed at Simone, who smiled in return.

On the dining room table was a decorative tray with a black ceramic pot of hot tea and matching cups. Cindy and the couple spoke in their native tongues, which Cindy later told Simone was Cantonese. The couple came to America in the early 1950s, and worked seven days a week at a local restaurant. They saved their money for ten years, and proudly opened their own Cantonese-style restaurant, which still exists today. Their three sons now run the restaurant. One son was married with children, and the two other boys still lived at home, caretakers to their aging parents. The elderly couple helped out at the restaurant on Christmas Day, and for two weeks during the Chinese New Year when the restaurant was extremely busy.

Simone allowed Cindy to take charge of the conversation. Simone nodding back at the couple. The woman poured cups of tea into the porcelain cups. It was served without sugar, honey or milk. Simone politely sipped the brew, which she found delicious.

Cindy translated to Simone that their only grandson was getting married next year. Tradition states that the groom's parents pay for the entire wedding, and they'd like to have the honor of doing so. Cindy further explained the couple would prefer having the wedding at a classy New York City hotel. They'd like Cindy to research which ones could satisfy their guest list of four hundred people, serve traditional Cantonese Roast Duck, and other specialty dishes. They were willing to provide some recipes for the occasion. The couple would pay for everything, including the bride's three dresses: a red dress, a traditional white wedding gown, and a ball gown. They agreed to pay for the couple's honeymoon.

Mrs. Lee left the table and returned a few minutes later with a brown grocery bag. She handed it to Cindy, bowed, and explained she and her husband had saved for this day for many years. Cindy looked inside the bag. She had no reaction. Or, as Simone preferred, it was a trained poker face. Inside the bag was $700,000 cash. Cindy tipped the bag to show Simone, who was speechless. She had never seen so much cash, and she wasn't sure it was a wise idea to walk the streets of New York City with the bag of money.

"There's more if necessary," the woman said in very broken English. "We pay."

Cindy closed up the bag and secured it into her messenger bag.

"Shouldn't we count the money before leaving?" Simone asked hesitantly.

"No need," Cindy answered. She lowered her voice, "I'd recommend we get a Town Car back to our office."

Simone punched in numbers on her cell phone. She was immediately notified that a driver would be there in twenty minutes.

"What about a contract?" Simone asked Cindy. "Or a receipt that we took this money?"

"It's all based on trust, Simone. It would be insulting to count it in front of them. If they said there's $700,000 in the bag, then that's how much there is. They apparently liked and trusted you to create a proper traditional wedding for their grandson. Obviously, if they didn't feel comfortable, they wouldn't allow you to leave their apartment with so much cash."

Simone turned to the couple. "We will do our very best to make you happy, and to present a wedding for your family that will be talked about for generations."

They respectfully bowed in unison.

Handshakes and hugs were exchanged as the two women left the building and got into the Town Car. Simone let out a sigh of relief when the driver got back into the car, locked the doors, and they headed towards the FDR Drive.

Simone said, "Driver, can you please put up the privacy glass?" When he stopped at the next traffic light, he turned away from the wheel, and Simone took the opportunity to put her finger to her mouth, indicating for Cindy not to say anything. After the partition was secured, Simone watched the driver's face through the rear view mirror for a reaction, and said, "I thought they were going to shoot you. I never expected them to pull a gun on you." No reaction at all by the driver. Simone was aware that some Town Cars and limousines were equipped with a microphone in the back, so the driver could listen in on conversations. Yes, it was an invasion of privacy, but there were times the driver's life was put in jeopardy.

"What was that all about?" Cindy asked.

"Sometimes the driver can hear your conversation. I just wanted to see what his reaction was."

"Oh. Good to know. Now, what are we going to do with all this cash?"

"When we get back to the office, I'll put it in the safe. It's too late to get to the bank today."

Simone turned and looked out the window, and watched the skyscrapers zipping by. After a few minutes she said, "Well, this was a first, Cindy. I never expected to be handed a bag of money."

"Not unusual for a couple like that. They don't trust many people, including banks. They pay cash for everything: food, utilities, insurance, etc."

"I had a feeling they understood everything I said."

Cindy nodded. "I know they understood you. I've known them most of my life, and they speak English fairly well. Again, it's a trust thing."

During the drive, Simone called Police Chief Cindy Jacobs of the Westport Police Department.

"Hi, Chief Jacobs. It's Simone Simpson."

"Ms. Simpson. How are you?"

"I'm fine, thank you. I'm wondering if you could have a policeman meet my associate and me outside my company at seven o'clock. We just met with a client who gave us a lot of cash, and we want to be sure nothing happens between the car and the office. We'll be in the black Town Car. And we'll need an officer to escort us to the bank tomorrow."

"Not a problem, happy to help."

"You know the Police Chief?" asked Cindy.

"There's a lot I need to share with you. Let's plan on breakfast tomorrow morning at the Sherwood Diner at seven-thirty. I'll fill you in on recent events, and some thoughts I have about your position in the company." Simone planned to discuss Cindy's lack of professional attire, but wanted to also show her support for securing a solid client. It would be a delicate conversation, but Simone felt a renewed sense of confidence in Cindy.

Simone made it a point to support the local police and firemen with holiday gift baskets, donations to their fundraisers, and an occasional arrangement of homemade cookies. They've helped her on more than one occasion, and she is appreciative of their hard work serving the community.

Chief Jacobs' police force saved Simone when she was in the middle of the home invasions, text messages from a burner phone, and the arrest of a perverted locksmith.

When the women arrived at Simone's business, there were two officers waiting for them.

"Is something wrong?" asked the driver when he saw the police.

"No, nothing at all. Thank you for driving us. Have a safe drive back." Simone gave him a generous tip. The two women exited the car, and entered "I Do" with the two police officers in tow.

Fifteen

The following morning, Simone and Cindy met at the Westport Sherwood Diner. Simone wanted to talk to Cindy before heading back to the office to count the money, and then deposit the cash in the bank.

Numerous tables were filled with people having early morning business meetings, as well as some teenagers either going off to work, or returning after an all-night party. Simone took a booth in the back of the diner, away from curious ears, and waited for Cindy to arrive.

She arrived wearing lululemon black yoga pants, a white sports top tied in the back at the waist, and ballet slippers. Patrons' eyes watched Cindy walk from the front door all the way to the booth where Simone was sitting.

The women ordered breakfast. Simone consumed above-normal amounts of coffee, while Cindy drank a cup of tea.

"The reason I wanted to meet, Cindy, is to give you some background information of how I run my company."

"From what I can see over the past few months, you run a tight ship."

"Yes, I do. I expect loyalty, absolute privacy about who we work with, and I don't want any personal problems brought to the office. We have enough drama dealing with bridezillas, motherzillas and entitled parents of overindulged twits . . . oops, sorry, I shouldn't have said that." She quickly corrected herself. "I meant, some children whom I think are overindulged by their parents. I'm serious, though about not bringing your personal life into the office."

"I understand. Katy gave me a heads up about that."

"Good. I want you to hear from me what happened with my former business partner, Jennifer Keys. Don't rely on what you've heard via office gossip, because I'm sure most of it isn't true." Simone proceeded to relay the entire gory story of her stalker, the roles and involvement of Jennifer and Charlie. "I don't want this repeated to anyone else in the office, or outside the workplace."

"Thank you for trusting me, Simone."

"You have the credentials. You've gone to the classes where you were taught about discretion, especially when it relates to high-end clients. One time, a famous actor walked into the company, and I thought Katy was going to faint. She acted like a teenager. He was flattered, of course, but also embarrassed. I gave her 'the look', and she went back to her seat. She apologized to me later, and realized her actions were unprofessional. No harm done. We did his wedding, which was very significant with a budget of $3.5 million."

Cindy stopped chewing and stared at Simone. "I'm very impressed, Simone. I knew your company got some high-end gigs . . ." Her words trailed off, fearing she'd say something insulting to Simone.

"We've worked weddings with even larger, and of course, much smaller budgets." Simone fixed another cup of coffee. She continued, "Speaking of being professional. Cindy, we need to discuss your attire. As I just said, I run a professional company with decorum. If another actor or actress walked into "I Do" and saw you dressed this way, I fear they'd turn around and walk back out."

Her words sat silently between them.

"I'm sorry, Simone. I thought you were joking a few weeks ago when you told me not to wear yoga pants to work. I won't do it again."

"In fact, Cindy. I want you to return home after breakfast and change your outfit."

Cindy stopped eating and cocked her head as to say, 'really?'

"We will be meeting with a policeman to escort us to the bank. We have a significant amount of funds that go through that bank." Simone withheld that the bank was also the recipient of millions of dollars of her personal money. "We must appear professional at all times no matter who we are seeing."

"I must say, Simone, I'm a little surprised, but I'll go home and change."

"You were dressed very appropriately and professionally yesterday, when we met with the Lees. That is exactly the correct dress protocol."

"Is there anything else you don't like about me?" Cindy asked.

"Cindy, what I'm saying is not a personal affront. It is constructive criticism. Please accept it as advice from a more experienced planner, and one who works with a very sophisticated and wealthy clientele. Things may be more casual in New York City, but not in my office. As you said, 'I run a tight ship.'"

Simone continued. "Later this afternoon, I have a meeting scheduled with a wealthy client. I'm going to talk to Katy ahead of time, because I don't want a repeat of when the actor came into the office. She is a well-known TV personality, with her own cooking show. She and her fiancé are getting married in a few months. She might have an entourage with her. After breakfast, I'm going to stop at The Chef's Table and pick up some nibbles. I'll tell Katy to offer coffee, and snacks. I want you to oversee that nothing goes amiss while I'm behind closed doors."

"So, you want me to play nursemaid?" Cindy snapped.

Simone didn't know how to respond. Was Cindy joking, or was she annoyed.

"No, I was thinking more that you'd be in charge of the office staff while I'm meeting with a client that has a two-million dollar budget. But, if that is not suitable for you, I'll give the job to Katy."

Simone realized Cindy wasn't Jennifer, either in professionalism or class, and she thought it wasn't fair to make a comparison.

"In this business," Simone said, "you have to be willing to be planner, consultant, babysitter, psychologist, and sometimes do jobs you feel are beneath you."

Cindy said nothing.

The conversation moved on to Gary "GG" Garrison. "I know you and GG don't get along very well, but do you think you'll be able to work with him to create the right atmosphere for the Lee wedding? We have a year to work on it, but I need to know if I'll need to bring in an outside designer."

"He is very good at what he does," Cindy said. "But his constant blabbering drives me crazy. And some of his bizarre design ideas are too much. To answer your question, I'll try to work with him."

"All right, then, I'll put him on the work schedule for that event. I'm glad you're able to put aside your feelings towards him. I intend to talk to him, as well. You're not the only one who has a problem with his personality. I agree, he's very good at what he does. He just needs to bring it down a notch."

Simone paid the bill, and they left the diner. Cindy drove back to her apartment and changed clothes, and Simone went to the office. After Cindy returned to the office, dressed appropriately, Simone called the Police Chief and requested the officer meet them at "I Do."

Within fifteen minutes, a female officer arrived. Simone opened the safe, removed the brown bag, and brought it into the conference room. There, behind a closed door, the officer watched while Simone and Cindy counted the money. Exactly $700,000. They put the bills into piles of $50,000, fastened each one with a rubber band, and it was returned to its brown bag. The three women walked outside to the police car. Cindy and Simone sat in the back while the officer drove them to the bank. Simone had called the branch manager before leaving the office, and gave him a heads-up they were coming with a large amount of cash to deposit into the business account.

The teller ran the money through the counting machine, deposited the cash, and gave Simone a receipt. Within the hour, Simone and Cindy were back in the office, returning phone calls and doing research. Simone informed Katy about the TV personality, scheduled to arrive at three o'clock, and that she expected nothing but professional behavior. "Please offer coffee and snacks to the couple, and to anyone else in their party."

Katy nodded.

The TV chef and her fiancé were dressed in torn jeans and Grateful Dead tee shirts, designer sunglasses and Mets baseball caps. They appeared nonchalant and low-key, and had only one additional person with them, a bodyguard.

They all stepped into the conference room. Katy gently knocked on the door and set out coffee and snacks, and quickly left without looking at the couple. She then offered the bodyguard the same amenities.

Simone secured the contract with the couple, assuring them complete confidentiality among her staff and crew.

"As you know, I can only do what I can to keep your wedding private," she said. "I'm sure you're followed all the time by the press. If any of them followed you here, they'll know you're planning an event, most likely your wedding."

"We let it drop that my mother is turning eighty, and we're planning a party for her. We'd like you to plan a Surprise Wedding. Do you know what that is, Simone?"

"Yes. Surprise Weddings have become quite popular as brides cannot tolerate the drama from families, bridal parties and guests. We organized one for another client. I'm sorry, I cannot give you their names, unless I ask them for permission. But I can tell you, they were extremely happy with the results."

They discussed dates, location, and what would be the "faux" occasion guests will be invited to attend. The wedding was to be next spring at a private yacht club on Cape Cod. Simone secretly hoped they wouldn't pick May nineteen, as that was the date of Judy Smith's wedding.

"We are thinking Mother's Day, May tenth. That's mom's birthday, and I know my relatives don't want to cook, or go to a restaurant. So having a party will be perfect."

"Agreed," Simone said.

She was suddenly overcome by a dizzy spell, but the couple didn't notice.

They spent the next fifteen minutes discussing details, and Simone promised to expand on the initial contract. Simone secured a contract for $2,000,000. The couple left Simone a check for $200,000 as partial payment.

Back to the bank, Simone thought.

All the while Cindy was seething with anger. *I bet she won't say anything to them about their clothes,* she thought.

Sixteen

At the weekly Thursday morning meeting, Simone updated her staff on future events, weddings, pending contracts, and cold calls. She said, "I'm happy to announce that Cindy secured a large four hundred guest wedding for next year. It will be a traditional Chinese wedding, and I'm asking all of you to educate yourselves on the protocol of such a wedding. We do not wish to insult our clients or their guests. Cindy will be more than happy to answer any questions."

She turned to GG. "Gary, I'd like to secure you for that wedding. You and Cindy will have to work closely together creating the perfect venue décor. Nothing tacky, of course."

"Like what?" GG asked.

"Like long strands of firecrackers, or anything offensive."

Cindy interrupted. "A fireworks show would be something the client might like, as well as a dance by a parade-sized lion. I've worked with a dance company who can provide the dancers. Of course, we need to include the traditional tea ceremony. I'll make a note to ask the Lees."

GG added, "There's a new craze in Chinese weddings – flying veils. It involves ceiling rails, weights and wire, but the results are very dramatic."

Cindy turned away from GG and rolled her eyes, which didn't go unnoticed by Simone.

"I read about the flying veil in one of the bridal blogs. Cindy can ask the clients if it is something they'd want," Simone said. "GG, do you want to explain what it is?"

"Sure," he answered excitedly. "The bride stands at the back of the ceremony venue, and the veil 'flies' across the room. When it is released, it lands on her head." He turned to Cindy and asked, "Can you see if the Lees would agree to this? If so, I'll start doing research plus do a test run."

"All great ideas," Simone interjected before Cindy had an opportunity to make a snide remark to GG. "Cindy, be sure you work with a reputable fireworks company that is licensed, and approved by both the venue and the town. The client has requested a hotel in New York City. You'll need to talk to the Lees about their flexibility, and if they're willing to go outside of New York City. We will have a lot of roadblocks trying to shoot off fireworks in New York City."

She continued. "Use your experience with these kinds of weddings to present options to the clients. Please run them by me as I might have some connections you can use."

Cindy responded, "Most of the Asian weddings I've done were at private homes in Queens or Long Island. A small fireworks show was usually over before someone called the authorities. Or, we shot off thousands of firecrackers as a celebration. Again, it was done outside, and we didn't need any permits."

"I will only do fireworks if we have permits," Simone said. "I have our reputation to protect."

Cindy put her head down, and along with GG, wrote notes.

"And I don't want any problems between the two of you. This is a very high end wedding. Everything must run smoothly without any drama. "Got it?" Simone asked looking at Cindy and Gary."

"Yes, boss." The two locked eyes.

Simone continued, "We also have a Surprise Destination Wedding next year on Mother's Day on Cape Cod. We organized one two years ago. If you need a refresher on the process, let me know. The guests will believe they're going to a birthday party for an eighty year old, when in fact, it will be a wedding. It is also a way to throw off the paparazzi. The couple is not willing to put up with the drama from people's opinions as to where the wedding should be, or when or who is sitting next to whom. They've both been married before, so they just want to keep it as simple as possible. We will handle the invitations, and responses."

"How big a wedding is it?" Katy asked.

"Seven hundred people," Simone answered. "And remember, the following weekend is Judy Smith's wedding. I'll need all hands on deck for that one as well."

"Who are they, Simone?" asked the receptionist.

"At this point, I'm not revealing their names. Let's just say she's a TV personality - a chef, and this wedding has to be kept a secret. If anyone leaks the information, and I find out, you'll be fired. Do I make myself clear?"

Boy, Simone has been grumpy lately, Katy noted. *I hope everything is okay with her and Charlie.*

Seventeen

On hot summer nights, Jennifer left work and drove directly to Silver Sands State Park, one of the many glorious beaches in town. Milford had over fourteen miles of shoreline along Long Island Sound, and Silver Sands was one of the many gems in the town.

There, she changed into sneakers and took a leisurely stroll along the boardwalk. This was her time to be alone, away from work, housekeeping, the dog, and Anthony. She knew that if she stopped at home first, Goober would want to be with her. She needed time to decompress, to think, to ponder life. It was during these alone moments that her thoughts drifted to Simone.

One late afternoon, Jennifer sat on a boardwalk bench, overlooking the crashing waves. Her focus turned to the numerous cairn sculptures. She watched a family building a new sculpture and listened to the children's laughter as the rocks collapsed amongst them. They gathered the stones, once again, and with hope and determination, would rebuild what nature destroyed.

The rocks ranged in size from a large pumpkin at the base to marble-sized stones on top. Balanced, one on top of another, they appeared from a distance as a rock cemetery.

They're balanced like a tower of strength, Jennifer thought. *They support each other. Simone . . . we once balanced and supported each other, too.* Their relationship crumbled, as if someone pushed over one of the rock sculptures. Her eyes teared and her throat tightened. But Jennifer quickly pushed away the feelings, convincing herself she didn't need Simone in her life. Or did she?

I wonder if I can rebuild what was destroyed, she mused.

Jennifer left the cairns and continued her walk until she reached the mouth of the tombolo leading to Charles Island. She looked out at the deserted fourteen acres filled with sparse trees. Legend has it, Captain Kidd buried his treasure on the island before heading up to Boston. Started in 2002, Milford celebrates this folklore with Pirates Day, held annually every June. There were remnants of an old monastery on the island, built by the Dominican Brothers who left the island in the 1930s. The monastery was destroyed during the major 1938 hurricane.

The tide was in, covering the enormous boulders that made up the walkway to the isolated island. When the tide ebbed, it exposed the tombolo like a walkway to a mysterious island. The walk was a challenge and extremely dangerous, as the path was slippery with irregular boulders, many covered with slimy, slick seaweed. A few tourists risked the trek past the first thirty or forty feet, but were forced to return to shore when they lost their footing, or felt the hike was more difficult than first realized. Fearless children approached the tombolo with determination, but once they fell and scraped their knees on a piercing edge of a boulder, they turned back searching for the comforting arms of their parents.

Firm equilibrium and concentration were required. Warning signs alerted the public to the dangers of crossing during high tide, which occurred two times a day. Such an attempt could result in severe consequences. Every year, a few people didn't heed the warnings and were swept out to sea, or miraculously, rescued by the coast guard.

In recent months, Anthony had become enthusiastic - almost obsessed - with going out to Charles Island. The island was closed to the public, surrounded by chicken wire from May to the end of August, to protect nesting birds, such as egrets, ibis and herons.

The back area of the island had an opening. Curious visitors, who did not heed the notices, used clippers to provide an entrance, away from the lifeguard's view from back on the beach.

Several times this summer, Anthony insisted that he and Jennifer go to the island to explore the terrain.

"But Anthony, both Charles and Duck Islands are closed to protect endangered birds."

"Fuck the ducks," he'd quip, disregarding the delicate state of the birds.

"That's an awful thing to say."

"You coming, or not?" he'd snap. "If not, I'm going by myself. You can come, or stay here and take care of Goober."

The dog whined at the sound of his name.

"Okay," she'd agree, although she hated herself for not standing up to his insensitivity.

Sometimes, they'd pack a light picnic and engage in a quickie in the woods. The thrill of being discovered by others excited Anthony, and his request for visiting the island increased to a manic level, concerning Jennifer.

Now that Jennifer was out of her half-foot high heels, her calves and toes cramped. She sat down, took off her sneakers and massaged her feet, hoping they wouldn't hurt walking back to her car.

"Wear high heels a lot?" a woman asked her, sitting down next to Jennifer.

"Yeah, how'd you guess?"

"It happened to me all the time. I don't wear heels any longer after my doctor explained they were ruining my feet."

"That's not something I'm willing to do," Jennifer said with a slight chuckle. "I own too many pairs of stilettos to give up on them. Besides, I don't want people to know how short I really am."

"I like your sense of humor," the woman said.

They introduced themselves to each other. "My name is Mary Ann Albano, and I live on Melba Street, on the corner of Platt."

"I know where those buildings are. They're apartments, right?"

"Condos," Mary Ann clarified.

"I live in a house not too far from you," Jennifer said. "Isn't it great living near the beach?"

"It's wonderful," agreed Mary Ann. "I love living where I am. I have two large bedrooms, two bathrooms, a spacious screened-in porch, and beach rights. It faces the water, and it's divine, especially this time of year. It's just shy of 1300 square feet."

"Wow. I had no idea the apartments over there were so large. Your apartment is bigger than my house," Jennifer said.

Before they left, they exchanged phone numbers, and promised to text when one of them planned to arrive at the beach. Jennifer and Mary Ann quickly became beach buddies, often meeting in the late afternoon, and walking the boardwalk together.

They discussed their respective lives. Mary Ann was married. She, a retired school teacher, loved to travel. Her husband, a motivational speaker, traveled frequently for business, and when possible, she'd join him. Fortunately, he could work from anywhere, enjoying the freedom of not being tied to a local job. Her parents are living in Florida, so Mary Ann and her husband spend the winters renting a place near them.

There was something about Mary Ann that made Jennifer feel comfortable. Eventually, she opened up about her frustrations with Anthony, and how she felt their relationship had hit a brick wall. She further announced that she hated her job, and wished she'd never left working with Simone at "I Do". She rattled on about the weddings they planned, how much fun they had together, but, because of Anthony, she had left "I Do".

Mary Ann asked, "Have you ever thought about calling Simone?"

"Yeah, all the time. Honestly, I'm afraid she'll hang up on me. Besides, she doesn't like Anthony, even though she's never met him. Sometimes I think I'm staying with him just to spite Simone."

"May I give you some unsolicited advice, Jennifer?"

Jennifer nodded.

"I'm older than you, and have seen and experienced a lot of different things. Life is short. One day you're a teenager, and the next, you're raising a teenager. But the core of a happy life has three parts: something to do, something to look forward to, and someone to love."

Mary Ann sat back allowing Jennifer to absorb her words.

Jennifer asked, "Who said that?"

"There's different theories. Some believe Elvis said it, but theologians believe Jesus was the first."

When Jennifer got home that evening she thought about what Mary Ann had said. She always had something to do, starting with cleaning up after Anthony or Goober. She rarely had something to look forward to . . . work . . . going home to Anthony and his mess. But, she did have someone to love. Anthony. Or did she?

Eighteen

The following day, Mary Ann texted she was leaving town with her husband for the weekend. *Have fun at the beach. I'll see you next week.*

Have a fun weekend. I look forward to seeing you on Monday, Jennifer texted back.

The walk at Silver Sands seemed lonely that day without her new friend. As she strolled, Jennifer realized she never told Anthony about Mary Ann. She decided Mary Ann would be a secret friend, not someone Anthony would try to keep her from . . . someone who would tell her to stay away from him . . . just like he did with Simone.

Jennifer didn't walk far that day. The air felt thick, and there wasn't an on-shore breeze. It was a typical mid-August afternoon, with triple-H weather: hot, humid and hazy.

She turned around and headed back towards her car. She was perspiring, and realized she was lonely without Mary Ann. Intense leg cramps forced her to find a place to sit. She took off her Keds and massaged her feet.

Seven years ago her doctor had warned her, "You have to stop wearing those pointy shoes and high heels. Start wearing sensible shoes, or, you're going to need foot surgery." But she ignored his advice, and continued to wear her trademark six inch heels.

Jennifer found an empty bench, closed her eyes, and let the warmth waft over her. She reflected on her life, and how it had changed over the last two years. She thought about Mary Ann's three essentials for happiness. *No,* she thought, *I am not happy.*

Her heartbeat increased as she thought about Simone. *Would she hang up on me if I called her? Did Simone miss me?*

Now, after all this time, it might be too late to reach out to her friend, and former business partner. Jennifer feared Simone had erased her from her life, and the two would never speak again. Were her concerns justified, or was she simply projecting Simone's reaction?

Jennifer's hand moved to her back pocket where she kept her cell phone. She lifted it out, scrolled through her contacts, but didn't see Simone's name. She looked under Simpson, "I Do" and searched under Charlie's name. No listings. *That's strange,* she thought. She must have deleted their information last year in a fit of anger. She pushed the phone back into her pocket, dismissing the disappearance of the names and phone numbers.

What Jennifer didn't know was that Anthony had erased and blocked Simone's name, number and email address from both her computer and her phone. He didn't want some smart-ass woman telling Jennifer not to be with him. No, he was in control of Jennifer - not Simone.

Her reverie continued.

Side by side with her friend and partner, they worked long hours creating and planning exclusive weddings and events, for which they got paid very well. Every wedding came with its own challenges and problems from entitled brides to dead members of the bridal party. But each wedding also brought great rewards, not only financially, but professionally. She and Simone had had fun together. More importantly, they trusted each other.

They were known as the dynamic duo of wedding planners in Fairfield County, Connecticut, booked years in advance by the wealthiest couples on the east and west coasts of the United States and Europe. Working with budgets over a quarter-million dollars, they, along with their team, would make the happy couples guests at their own weddings; hiding any behind-the-scenes problems. They spent endless hours with couples discussing every aspect involved with planning a wedding.

Jennifer missed the fast-paced work, the pressure of satisfying every minute detail, and successfully providing the couple and their guests a wedding they would never forget. These days, Jennifer's work was spent convincing people to buy her company's drugs, fighting off the advances of the salesmen, and something else . . . what it was . . . she wasn't sure. She let her mind drift, but something nagged at her. What was it that bothered her, what made her feel sad, lost and unfulfilled? Was she just missing Simone? Or, was there another force occupying her mind?

Have something to do, something to look forward to and someone to love. These words haunted her and permeated her mind.

Her eyes suddenly grew wide. She sat up straight and her mouth dropped open. The word 'no' softly emanated. It was a whisper, but anyone sitting close by would have heard it.

She knew what it was. She shook her head. It wasn't possible. An epiphany --- one she refused to acknowledge or accept, hit her with such force it frightened her. She glanced yards away at the cairn sculptures. An energy seemed to pull her towards the rocks. She understood now. The towers were analogous to her life, Jennifer thought. They stood strong, but could easily crumble with the slightest push. Only those that were grounded into the earth by nature belonged together, not those created by people who *thought* they belonged together.

Feelings she never thought possible, suddenly surfaced. They can't be right, she tried to convince herself. No, they can't be.

Jennifer tied her Keds, stood up, and began walking quickly towards her car, ignoring the pain in her feet and legs. Her heart pounded. How could she be so stupid . . . so blind . . . so foolish. Her mother's words resurfaced: "Play with a wild cat and the devil will eat you." Jennifer dismissed this as an Irish proverb. But now, she understood its meaning.

Tears sprung forth and rolled down her cheeks. She missed her mother whom she hadn't spoken to in several weeks. Her mother didn't like Anthony, and said so in their last conversation.

"Jennifer, he has eyes of the devil," she had said.

"You say that about every guy I date," Jennifer retorted. "No one is good enough for you."

"My child," her mother had said trying to keep an even tone in her voice, "I don't want you to make a mistake. You say you love this boy, and you're going to get married. But where's the ring? Why haven't you set a date? Yet, you give him your money to buy a house. Jennifer, look at your cousin, Sylvia's daughter . . ."

"I'm not her," Jennifer snapped. "She got pregnant and had to marry that idiot. Mom, stop telling me what to do. I'm thirty years old, and I can make my own decisions. I have to go." And she had hung up.

Now she wished she could take it all back.

Jennifer reached her car, got in, and before the door slammed shut, she began sobbing. Deep heaving cries of regret, mixed with tears of anger at herself.

She knew what she had to do to fix her life. The first thing was to call her mother and apologize. She'd drive out to Long Island and spend the weekend with her and try to make amends. If her mother had handled her father differently, and had set a better example as a role model, Jennifer's life might have turned out differently, too.

Similarly, if Jennifer had demanded that Anthony pick up his wet towels, and do his own laundry, and take care of his dog . . . and cook a meal every once in a while . . . she realized she was just like her mother . . . she, too, was an enabler.

Again, her thoughts turned back to Simone. "Oh God," she said out loud as fresh tears appeared. With all her heart Jennifer wished Simone was sitting next to her now so she could apologize, and tell her friend how much she missed her. She wanted to share her feelings, her fears, and her mistakes. And ask for forgiveness of her friend. More importantly, of herself.

Nineteen

On Tuesday afternoons, Francine watched her grandchild while her daughter went shopping or had her nails done. She left the toddler sleeping in the portable crib in the finished basement, and returned upstairs to the family room to watch her soap operas. She turned on the baby monitor in the kitchen, in case the baby stirred.

Fifteen minutes later, she heard a voice coming from the small box in the kitchen.

"How's my little munchkin?"

It was a woman's voice, but not her daughter's. Fran ran down the flight of stairs, nearly tripping. She rushed to the crib. Her grandchild was sound asleep.

Where did the voice come from, she wondered? She returned to the kitchen and turned off the monitor, then on again, thinking there was an electrical short. There was that woman again, offering the child a bottle. The voice sounded vaguely familiar, but the static and the woman's singsong tone, made it difficult to decipher.

It's the damnedest thing, Francine thought. *Who the hell was talking?* Suddenly, there was loud crackling and the voice disappeared.

She looked out the kitchen window and searched for a worker on a utility pole, or a cable company truck, but she didn't see anyone. She opened her front door, stepped onto the stoop, and looked up and down the street. Again, there weren't any utility workers around. She closed the front door, and diligently turned the deadbolt.

Francine had noticed Veronica's car in the parent's driveway, but that wasn't unusual. The girl was always there. Francine decided she'd ask her husband if he could solve the mystery.

She could ask Vinny when he got home. He was taking computer classes at night. Maybe he would know how baby monitors worked. She reconsidered the idea, and decided it might be a good way to hear what was going on in Tara's house. This would be another secret she'd keep close to her heart.

Twenty

"Hey, Anthony, what's wrong?" asked Felix, his co-worker. "You've been looking depressed for the past couple of weeks. Everything okay?"

"Yeah, I guess," Anthony said in a tone that invited further questioning. Felix took the bait.

"Want to talk about it?"

"Just stuff going on at home," he said. "It's kind of personal, man, and I'm not sure you'd want to hear about it."

Felix, a confirmed bachelor, thrived on his friend's woes, proving to himself that his carefree life was one his friends should envy. He was relieved he didn't have to deal with drama from a girlfriend, a wife, or kids. He had relocated to New York City from Iowa, and was living a wild life. "I'm sowing my oats," he told his co-workers and friends.

"If you want to talk, I'm here," said Felix. "I probably can't give you any good advice, because I stay away from romance problems. But if you're having car trouble, I'm your guy."

"Well, I really don't have anyone to talk to about this," Anthony confessed, a bit shyly. "I told my brother, but he's no help." He paused and then said, "It's about Jennifer, my girlfriend. I think she's cheating on me."

"No way, man," said Felix, his interest piqued. "You said she was loyal as a puppy."

"Yeah, well I thought so, too, but lately she's been coming home late. And sometimes, she smells like cigarettes, like she's been at a club or something."

"Have you asked her about it?"

"No. I don't want her to think I'm jealous. She told me that salesmen at work are always asking her out. She's also not so interested in sex these days. And she's been picking fights over stupid things. Like the other morning, I left my coffee cup in the sink. She got on me for not putting it in the dishwasher."

"That's why I stay away from chicks," said Felix. "They think they own you when you live with them. If I want to leave my coffee cup around, I ain't got no bitch getting all mad at me. But that seems like a minor thing to get upset about."

"That's what I mean. It's stupid shit she's nagging me about. Like maybe she wants to start a fight, so we would break up."

Felix thought for a moment, then continued giving his unworldly advice. "You know why most of the people on the TV show about Mayberry were happy? Because none of them were married, except Otis, the town drunk. And you know how he felt about having a wife. Everyone else: Andy, Barney, Gomer and Floyd were unmarried. Even Aunt Bee was single, and she always had a smile and a happy song to sing."

Anthony thought about his dog, Goober. Did he, unconsciously, give the animal a name from one of the happy characters on that show? He adopted the dog at a pet-adoption day. An enormous van was parked in the lot near Wal-Mart. People were lined up to adopt cats, dogs, rabbits and other four-legged creatures. Anthony casually walked past the van, saw a dog sitting next to a worker, and locked into the mutt's pleading eyes, which seemed to say: *Take me home. Please.*

The multi-colored black and white pup had enormous paws, and a tail that never stopped wagging. Globs of snot hung from its nose. The vet spotted Anthony staring, and came in for the sales pitch.

"What's wrong with him?" Anthony asked.

"He has a sinus infection, but he's on the mend. He's a very sweet dog, very loving, and good with kids. If you adopt him, we'll give you his medicine, two follow-up examinations, a collar and leash, and plenty of dog food. He'll need to be neutered in a few months, and we'll give you a coupon for a discount."

She added, "He likes you."

Anthony put his hand out for the dog to sniff, and was immediately covered with slimy goobers, hence the name Anthony chose.

A technician handed Anthony paper towels to dry his hand. Then the dog looked up at Anthony and barked. It was a squeaky-sounding bark.

"His throat is a little sore from the sinus drainage. I'm sure his bark will get better with time. He was found roaming the streets in Bridgeport, skinny, covered with fleas and eating from a garbage can. He . . ."

"I'll take him," Anthony said impulsively, interrupting the vet. "And I'm naming him Goober."

Felix interrupted Anthony's reminiscing. "I can't give you any advice, man. Maybe follow her, or something. See if she's meeting up with some other guy." He ended with, "Glad I'm not in your shoes."

"Thanks for listening, Felix. I really appreciate it," Anthony said, wondering if Felix was even buying his story.

This same fabricated tale was told to several of Anthony's friends, either by him or through the gossip train. He needed others to believe Jennifer was cheating on him. That was crucial to him.

A week later, Anthony suggested that he and Felix go out after work for a few drinks. "I need to talk to you, man. But not here. Let's meet for burgers at SBC downtown."

In the restaurant, Anthony told his co-worker his newest tale of woes. "I took your advice and followed Jennifer. Yeah, she's got a guy on the side. It's weird, he sort of looks like me. He's around my height, and dark-haired like me. I swear, I thought I had another twin. It was freaky, man."

Felix said empathetically, "I'm sorry to hear about your woman troubles, Anthony. I really am. Do you think you're going to move out?"

"I'm not moving out," Anthony said adamantly. "She's the one who's cheating, so she can move. Jennifer still has an apartment in Fairfield, so she can stay there. The problem is we own the house together, so if we split up, I'll have to buy her out."

"Maybe just talk to her, and tell her you know what's going on."

"I'll wait until I catch her red-handed, or when she says she wants to break up."

They ate their burgers and fries, and had two IPO beers each. Anthony belched, leaned back against the booth and announced, "I sure could go for some serious drinking. And some entertainment." He looked around, sure no one was within earshot and whispered, "Want to go to a club where a friend of mine dances?"

"Sure," Felix said. "Won't Jennifer get upset if you're not home?"

Anthony's mind raced to come up with an answer. "She's at an expo in Atlantic City. She's gone for a couple of days. I'll text my mom and ask her to walk my dog." Anthony took out his cell, pretended to be texting his mother. Then he airdropped the address of *The Cat's Meow* to Felix's phone. "I'll meet you there."

At *The Cat's Meow*, Fran danced her magic, paying extra attention to Felix. The two men had four rounds of boiler makers, before the bartender slowed down their refills.

"I don't understand," slurred Felix. "You're upset that your woman is getting something on the side, but you have this one as a *friend*," he said as he pointed up at Fran. "I have a new opinion of you." He lowered his voice and asked, "You banging her?"

Anthony looked up at Fran and took a good look at her body. Then, looked back at Felix with a sly grin on his face. "She's got lots of cushion for the pushin'."

"You're terrible." Then he lowered his voice and asked, "What about Jennifer?"

"What she don't know, won't hurt her," Anthony slurred back. They slapped each other a high five. "What's good for the goose . . ."

"Last call," the bartender announced. "Want me to call you guys a cab?"

"Presto," yelled Felix looking at Anthony, "You're a cab." The two men laughed.

"Or, I can call the cops to escort you dudes home."

The men stopped laughing. "We're okay," Felix said. They got up and staggered out of the bar.

"Where'd I park my car?" Felix asked looking up and down the deserted street.

"Don't you remember? You left your car at home and walked here."

"Oh, yeah. Man, I'm wasted. Where's your car?" Felix slurred.

"I put it in the muni lot. It'll be okay until tomorrow," Anthony assured Felix.

They left the bar and wandered the streets. Felix stopped in front of a tattoo shop. "Ain't it late for the shop to be opened?" Felix asked through his brain fog.

"Lots of guys get tats after a night of partying. Even the chicks," Anthony said, knowingly.

"Hey, let's get a tat to remember the night." Felix egged Anthony on.

After a nanosecond, he shouted, "Yeah. Let's go for it."

While an artist created a design on Felix's forearm, another artist asked Anthony, "What'll be, pal?"

Trying to focus through his inebriated state, he said, "I don't know. I don't want it to show. What do you suggest?"

"How about 'Mom' tattooed on your ass," the proprietor chuckled. "Or, the name of your girlfriend."

Felix suggested, "Hey man, how about that hottie?"

"Yeah," Anthony replied.

The tattoo artist went to work, and by the time he was finished, there was a thin, black outline of a heart with her name permanently tattooed on Anthony's left butt cheek.

"Now her name is close to your heart," the artist chortled.

The men walked to a 24-hour diner where they ate three-egg omelets, home fries, toast, and drank multiple cups of coffee.

"Just leave the pot, toots," Felix said to the waitress in a flirty tone.

"You're drunk," she answered flatly, and walked back to her station along with the coffee pot.

Anthony stumbled back to his car, drove Felix to his apartment a few blocks from the bar, and then drove the three miles to his cottage. It was four-thirty a.m., and the sky was displaying its early morning purple hues. He dropped his clothes on the floor, and was asleep as soon as his head hit the pillow. He awoke the next afternoon at one o'clock, with a raging hangover. He had no recollection of the night before, didn't know where he had been, or even how he got home.

He turned over, but Jennifer wasn't in bed. He heard pots clanking downstairs. When he tried to sit up, his head pounded, his tongue and teeth felt as if coated with lamb's wool, and he had a sore left butt cheek. He stumbled to the bathroom and looked in the mirror. He had deep dark circles under his eyes, and wasn't surprised to see his tongue had a white coating. He turned and looked at his backside in the mirror. He almost screamed when his eyes locked on the angry-red tattoo of a heart with the name Fran permanently branded into his skin. "Shit," he said out loud.

Taking a shower was painful, drying his butt cheek, even more. He needed time to concoct a story before going downstairs to face Jennifer. She was bound to have seen the tattoo.

"Good morning, Anthony. Or, should I say, good afternoon," Jennifer said with a chill in her voice. She stood at the stove cooking old fashioned oatmeal for him. She didn't turn around.

"Good afternoon, babe," he said as he kissed her neck. "Sorry I came home so late last night."

Jennifer didn't answer. She scooped a glob of oatmeal into a bowl. The sight of the thick beige matter almost made Anthony retch. She walked to the table and placed the dish down. "Eat the oatmeal," she encouraged. "It will help with the hangover."

Anthony sat down and emitted an "ouch" from the pain. He stared at the oatmeal, then forced a small teaspoon of the mass into his mouth. Bile rose up, refreshing his memory of greasy home fries, eggs and burnt coffee. He drank the full glass of orange juice Jennifer placed in front of him. He took another spoonful of oatmeal, and prayed the food would stay down.

Jennifer put three aspirins in front of Anthony, which he consumed with a refill of orange juice. She placed the juice container in front of him.

"Thanks, babe. You're so good to me."

"Cut the crap, Anthony. I'm not buying your pathetic story. Where were you last night?" she demanded.

He drained his cup of coffee before speaking. "Babe, we need to talk."

"I'm listening," she said, sitting down across from him, her hands cupped around a mug of coffee.

"I have something to tell you, and I think you're going to be very upset with me," Anthony said with a sheepish look on his face.

"More upset than you coming home at four-thirty this morning?"

He said, "I did something last night that I'm ashamed of, and I hope you'll forgive me."

Jennifer put down her coffee mug, a stream of fear mixed with rage coursed through her body. He came home smelling of alcohol and antiseptic. She assumed he had vomited somewhere, and purchased a bottle of mouthwash at the local 24-hour 711. It wouldn't be the first time he thought he could disguise the smell of excessive drinking from his breath. Unfortunately, the odor, like excessive eating of garlic, oozed from his body.

"I went out with a bunch of guys from work," he lied. "I got very drunk, and I did something that I'm afraid to tell you. I think you're going to be very angry."

Jennifer assumed he spent the night with another woman.

"So, did you sleep with someone else?" she asked coldly.

"No, babe. Of course not. I would never do that," he said unconvincingly. "Something worse."

Immediately, she thought he killed someone with his car while driving drunk . . . got arrested . . . was mugged . . . a long list of scenarios ran through her mind.

"Anthony, whatever happened, you can tell me. It can't be so horrendous that we can't discuss it. We're a couple now, and we need to be able to tell each other anything."

Anthony almost puked at her words, but kept his emotions under control. He took another scoop of oatmeal and drowned it down with gulps of orange juice.

"It's really serious," he continued, flawlessly playing the role of victim. "I'm not sure you'll understand. I'm not sure I understand it myself."

"Anthony, just tell me," Jennifer said, her anxiety increasing. *Did he really do something horrible, or is he building up to something stupid?* she wondered.

He stood up and started to unbuckle his pants. Jennifer thought he was going to show her a herpes sore . . . a belly ring . . . or manscaping. She didn't know what to expect. Unless he wanted to have sex.

He dropped his pants and underwear, pushed them aside, and faced her.

"Now, Anthony? You want me to satisfy you, now?"

"No, babe. I'm afraid you'll freak when I show you what I did," Anthony said, his eyes downcast. Slowly, he turned and revealed his left butt cheek.

Jennifer burst out laughing. "Anthony, you have no idea what I thought you were going to show me. I'm not thrilled that you had your mother's name tattooed to your ass. A little Oedipus complex - but that's all? You had me worried."

A bolt of reality hit him. *Fuck- it's my mother's name!*

He refocused. "Oh babe, you're the best," he said as he grabbed Jennifer into a bear hug. He kissed her passionately. "Since I'm undressed . . . what do you say . . . kiss your baby's boo-boo?"

"You're still drunk," she quipped, and pushed him away. "Your breath smells like a still. When you sober up, we need to talk."

"As soon as I can, I'll have it removed by laser," Anthony said. "But I think I'll have to wait a few months before it's completely healed. Just don't tell anyone. You promise? I'm not going to tell Vinny, because he'll torture me for the rest of my life."

"Your secret is safe with me," she promised.

Twenty-One

Vinny and Angie had been dating since high school, when he was a senior, and she was a junior. Now at twenty-eight, she nagged Vinny about getting married. He, like his brother, preferred the luxury of having his mother take care of his household needs, and Angie, his sexual needs. He also didn't want to give up sexual liaisons with Joannie, when she was able to get away from her abusive husband.

"Shit, why should I buy the cow if I get the milk for free?" he once said to Anthony. "I think Angie's bored, and wants to set up house and have kids. She said she won't live with me unless there's a ring on her finger. She doesn't want to be like Jennifer."

"Yeah, Jennifer is bitching about the same thing. I told her we'll get married next year. That was the only way I could get her to pay for half the house. She was complaining the other day that I treat her like mom . . . making her do all the work in the house. So I banged the shit out of her, and told her that's not how I treat mom."

Vinny laughed. "You're such a pig." Vinny paused for a few moments before he whispered, "Is she any good?"

"Yeah, she's good. Goober thinks I'm killing her, so we have to lock him out of the bedroom. She's a screamer."

"No shit. Hey, bro. Want to do a swap?" Vinny asked.

Anthony thought about this for a few moments, recalling the times they did this to several women. Anthony remembered the tattoo and said, "No, it was fun in high school and college, but not now, Vin. Jennifer would know it wasn't me. Don't you think Angie would know, too?"

Vinny answered, "Nah, she's just happy to get laid. Although, she might get suspicious if you do things to her that I hate to do." The two brothers continued talking smack, and laughed with disregard and disrespect for their girlfriends.

But the conversation put an idea in Anthony's mind: *A swap.* The thought intrigued him.

Twenty-Two

"Hi ma," Anthony and Vinny announced in unison.

"Oh, what a nice surprise," Francine said as she closed the door behind the twins. "What brings you here? Ant, you'll stay for dinner?"

"I came to play some video games. Sure, I'll stay for dinner. I'll text Jen and let her know."

"I'm about to start watching my stories," Francine said. "You boys go downstairs, and I'll call you when dinner is ready." She spoke to them as if they were ten years old.

Keeping one eye on the television, she removed a frozen container of gravy with meatballs, and a salad mix from the refrigerator. As she tore salad leaves into a bowl, she smiled at having her sons back in the house.

Her mind wandered back to her daughters and her grandchildren. Her eldest, Cathy had three boys ages three to nine. Her other daughter, Margaret, had two little girls, eight and ten. And Theresa had a newborn girl. She wished Vinny and Anthony would settle down and start to raise their own families. She wanted more grandchildren.

In the basement the grandkids played Wii board games, cards, or with Francine's old Barbie dolls. And when they played or napped, Francine turned on the baby monitor. Sometimes she had to run down to break up fights over dolls, or acted as referee as to whose turn it was at a video game.

Although the boys were thirty years old, and she knew it was an invasion of privacy, she was curious to know what her sons discussed.

She was downright nosey. She felt entitled to know what was being said in her home. Her sixty-fifth birthday was three months away, and she secretly wished they were in the basement planning her surprise party. *After all, I always gave them parties. Now, it's my turn.* She put the television volume on mute, turned on the monitor, and listened.

"So, how do you see this going down?" Vinny asked.

"A surprise for sure."

Francine's ears perked up, a smile forming on her face.

"When are you thinking?" Vinny questioned.

"Before Labor Day, during the week on a Tuesday. The closer to sunset, the better."

During the week? Francine was confused by what she heard.

"Do you know where you want to do this?" Vinny asked.

"Yeah, Charles Island."

Charles Island. No one from my family, or my friends will be able to get out to Charles Island. Are these boys crazy?

"Yeah, the water is wild out there, Anthony said. "We've been out numerous times, so I don't think she'll get suspicious. When the chart shows low tide in the afternoon, we meet at Silver Sands. As you know, it's tricky getting out there. It's now closed off to the public because of some friggin' birds nesting out there. In the back of the island there's a cut in the chicken wire. Go in there, and you'll be able to walk around."

Francine dragged a chair from the table, and sat down at the counter, closer to the monitor. *They can't be planning my birthday party.*

Anthony continued revealing his plan. "I've thought this out, Vin. You'll meet her at Silver Sands at our usual spot in front of the tombolo. Bring some snacks and small boxes of wine. Steal one of mom's Xanax and put it in her wine ahead of time. That'll knock her out. Once the drug takes effect, get your ass off the island. Leave, and meet me at Stonebridge."

Anthony continued to reveal his plan. "Buy a waterproof cover for your cell phone. You can leave a change of clothes in your car. Change, and meet me at the bar. We'll have to check the tides and the weather ahead of time. We might have to move the plan by a day or two, or even a week."

"Do you think only one of mom's pills will do it?"

"Good point. On second thought, grab two. You and I will go out there, and I'll show you our special place," Anthony said with a grin. "That's where we go for a quickie."

"You're a pig, Ant. A real pig."

"Yeah, and she loves it."

After a few thoughtful moments, Vinny asked, "Hey, if I get her out there, can I screw her?" he asked wringing his hands like a big bad wolf. "Let her go out with a smile on her face."

Anthony laughed, then suddenly remembered the tat on his ass. She'd know it was Vinny. Anthony quickly added, "On second thought, bro, don't have sex with her. It's enough we're going to off her. I feel bad her body won't be found for a while, no need to leave her there naked."

"Okay, Ant. I get it. I won't touch her," though he had other ideas.

Anthony hoped his brother believed his pathetic story. More importantly, he needed to trust that his brother would honor his promise. He continued, "After the deed is done, call me at work. Then, hit FaceTime so the people in the office – witnesses – will know you're calling me. You'll say you're at work, and I'll ask you to meet me and Felix at Stonebridge."

Meanwhile, upstairs in the kitchen Francine began feeling sick. Her stomach lurched, her head pounded, and her eyes welled up. She heard what her sons were saying, but was in disbelief that they could devise such a horrific plan.

"Will she be able to get off from work?" Vinny asked.

"During the summer, her schedule is more flexible. She can tell her boss she has a meeting or something. We have plenty of time to figure that out. I've been telling guys at work that I think she's cheating on me, so even if the lifeguards or beachgoers see you two going out there, they'll think she's with her lover, and not me, or you, because you'll be at work."

"You know, for the dumb twin, you're pretty smart," Vinny joked.

"Frig you, asshole," Anthony said as he threw a pillow at his brother.

Francine wondered if her boys were merely concocting a prank. They weren't diabolical. *Maybe they know I'm listening in on the baby monitor, and they're saying these things just to tease me,* she thought.

Anthony continued, "She's not a good swimmer, only looks good in a bikini. I swear, if she wore those heels in her bathing suit, she could compete for Miss America."

Francine was dumbfounded. They were not planning her surprise sixty-fifth birthday party, after all. No, they were planning something evil and sinister. "Oh my God," she muttered, and quickly cupped her hand across her mouth. *They're talking about Jennifer. They're going to kill her.*

Vinny inquired, "Ant, what do you expect to gain from all of this?"

Anthony lowered his voice to a whisper, forcing Francine to put her ear closer to the monitor.

"Remember when we went to the attorney when Jennifer and I purchased the house?" His brother nodded. "Well, at that meeting, I asked him if we should get a will. Since we weren't married at the time, what would happen if one of us died; would the other one get the house, or would our parents get it? I told him we were planning to get married in the near future, and I didn't want anything to happen to my girl. The lawyer suggested we draw up wills, naming each other as beneficiaries. Ready for this – he also suggested we get life insurance policies. Holy crap. It's like he was reading my mind. If something happens to me, she'll get money to carry the house, making up the money she'd lose in the future without my income. And I'll get the payout on her policy. Cool, huh?"

"And she agreed to this?"

"At first, she balked. I told her that on my salary alone, I couldn't cover the expenses of the house. We're both young so the insurance payments are low. If I croaked, she'd lose my future earnings. And if she croaked, I couldn't carry the house by myself. Finally, she agreed to go for a physical and take out the life insurance policy. She went for two million dollars."

"No friggin' way," Vinny shouted.

"She said, 'the way you drink and drive, you'll probably die first.' It gets even better. She has life insurance from her company. A small policy of $10,000 to cover funeral expenses."

"That's a ton of money, bro."

"There's more. When she quit working for that bitch, Simone, she got a payout of $375,000 to walk away. She was a partner in the firm."

"Oh, my God!" Vinny shouted.

"Shh. You don't want ma to hear us." Anthony lowered his voice. "The best part is I never went for the physical, and didn't take out a policy on myself. I ain't goin' nowhere. Not planning to die anytime soon." Anthony guffawed, "She's so gullible. So when she's gone, I'll get the house, the life insurance money, the $375,000, any money she has in the bank, all of her shoes, too. They're probably worth a few grand. I'll probably walk away with well over two and a half million. And, as I promised, Vinny, I'll share the money with you."

"We'll have to figure out a way to hide the money from the Feds," added Vinny, trying to sound like he knew what he was talking about. "Maybe we can start a shell company; like we're going into business together. I've seen that on TV. People do it all the time. We'll put the money there, and siphon off what we need."

"How will you get your hands on the money?" Vinny asked, concerned.

"I just need to show the insurance companies a death certificate, and it's all mine," Anthony said with confidence. "Easy-peasy."

The brothers did not know that a dead body had to surface in order to obtain a death certificate. For someone who is missing, and never recovered, they might have to wait seven years before the person could be legally claimed deceased.

Vinny took out his brown notebook, and began making a list of things to research, including details. Anthony would check the tide charts. They'd practice doing the phone call, and even do a walk out to Charles Island, if necessary, before the actual planned incident.

All this while Francine kept her ears peeled. She knew she would be in danger if they discovered she had overheard their conversation. She shut off the monitor, and quickly wrote a note. She went to her bedroom, pulled down the shades, drew the draperies, and got under the covers.

Her mind raced anxiously. *Do I tell their father? Johnny would kill them if he knew what his sons were planning. Maybe I should talk to Father Bennett. Would he tell someone, even though he is vowed not to reveal what he hears in a confessional? Should I warn Jennifer?* She wrestled with her thoughts.

This last thought brought a guilt-ridden smile to her face. *If their plan works, it'll be a good way to get rid of that entitled, good for nothing girl. Maybe Anthony would then get himself a nice Italian girl, instead of an offspring from alcoholics.*

When the boys didn't hear a call for dinner by seven, they went upstairs, and found the note on the kitchen table:

Got one of my migraines. Sorry, you'll have to fend for yourselves.

"Gee, ma must be feeling really bad, she didn't cook for us," said Vinny. "Do you think she heard us?"

"I doubt it," said Anthony. "If she did, she would have come downstairs and smacked us on the side of the head."

Vinny scribbled: *Feel better. V&A*

Then, they left the house and drove to Mama Teresa's Restaurant. Over beers and a pizza, they reviewed their plans. As they gathered more information, Vinny wrote it down in his diary. They ate and drank as they searched their phones for tide chart information.

"There's low tide at three o'clock on Tuesday, August twenty-seventh. That's good. If we . . . I mean, you . . . get her out to the island. It takes about an hour to get out there. When you arrive, have your food, and then drug her. She'll be out cold in less than half an hour.

Leave the island right away, and you'll make it to Stonebridge before six. She'll sleep for a few hours, and wake up in time for high tide. It'll be dark and the next low tide ain't until the next morning. We can hope she tries then. In the dark, she won't have a prayer for getting back, and she'll get swept out to sea. Never to be heard from again."

And if I'm lucky, Anthony thought, *you'll get swept out too, so I won't have to share my fortune.*

"What if she figures out it's me, and not you. She might try to run, and get off the island before I drug her."

"I don't know. Keep your sunglasses on and wear one of my baseball caps. The sun is strong from that angle, so she won't get suspicious. The fewer people who see your face, the better."

"Won't she get suspicious if she notices the tide coming in?"

"Naw, she'll believe what I tell her. I'm telling you, she's gullible."

"How do you plan on having her body found?" Vinny asked. "That sounds like an important thing, don't you think? And what if they find her body right away, how are you going to convince the cops you weren't with her?"

"I've been thinking about that," Anthony said. "As I told you, I've been telling people at work and my poker buddies I think Jennifer is cheating on me. I've been finding little clues, like she has a lot of after-work meetings, she's been a little distant. I'll make it sound like she's got someone on the side. I'll play the poor victim. So, if my friends are interviewed by the police, they can say I suspected there was someone else."

"I don't think you should text her, Ant. That could be used as evidence. Tell her the day before to meet you. She might blab to someone at work that you two are going to Charles Island for a picnic. You're going to have to be real careful how you handle this. And what about her car? If she leaves it in the parking lot, the State Police will find it when the park closes."

"For the dumb twin, you ain't so stupid," Anthony quipped.

Vinny picked off a slice of pepperoni from the pizza and threw it at Anthony. "Frig you," he said in a raised voice.

Disapproving looks came from two elderly ladies sitting across from them.

"Sorry, ma'am," Vinny said. "It's just that my brother is a jerk."

The two women turned back to their conversation, shaking their heads and whispered their disapproval of the younger generation's lack of respect. And for the conversation they overheard. They might be old, but they weren't deaf or dumb.

"Do you think they heard us?" Vinny asked slanting his head towards the two women sitting across from them.

"Naw. They're just a bunch of old ladies. They're probably hard of hearing," Anthony said, his voice lowered.

Another look passed between tables, answering Vinny's question.

Dropping his voice to a whisper, Vinny said, "I think they heard you."

"Too bad," Anthony mumbled. "Ignore them."

The two brothers continued discussing their plans, the tide chart, and the best day to complete their mission. It was set: Tuesday, August twenty-seventh. Vinny was to meet Jennifer at three o'clock at the sandbar.

"I'm worried about ma," Vinny said. "It's not like her not to leave something for us. No matter how sick she is, she always manages to leave food for me and dad. I really hope she didn't hear us," he reiterated.

"How could she have heard us? We were in the basement and she was upstairs watching her shows. She couldn't have heard us," Anthony said.

"Unless . . . she . . ." Vinny stopped mid-sentence.

"What?" Anthony asked.

"What if she turned on the baby monitor? She's always got that thing on when the kids are over," Vinny said.

"She wouldn't do that when we're downstairs," Anthony rebutted. "She only uses it for the grandkids, not us. You're becoming paranoid, bro."

"She didn't fix us any food. I'm really concerned ma wasn't sick at all. When she's mad at dad she'll go upstairs with one of her so-called headaches, but she'll always leave him a dish of food he could nuke. She never goes upstairs without cooking something. I think she heard us, Ant."

"Let's see if she starts acting weird around us. If she doesn't look us in the eye, or starts asking about Jennifer, we'll know."

"Well, what are we going to do if she did?"

The two boys were thinking the same thing, but neither one was willing to say the words out loud.

Anthony cracked his knuckles. "We got ourselves out of jams before; we'll get out of this one. Don't worry, bro, no one heard us."

Except for the two matching baby monitors.

Twenty-Three

Quite by a terrifying accident, Tara Palmieri discovered that the baby monitor she got from Francine also picked up conversations at her sister-in-law's house next door.

Veronica had left her mother's home to get a haircut, a pedicure and manicure - a day of beauty, she indulged in every three months. Tara put her grandchild down for a nap in Veronica's childhood bedroom. "You go to sleep now and when you get up, Grandma Ta-ta will have a nice bowl of pastina for you."

Tara left the bedroom and walked down the hallway to the kitchen. She turned on the monitor to listen to her granddaughter babble before falling off to sleep. As she stood at the sink scraping the skin from a hothouse cucumber, she heard a woman's voice singing a lullaby. She shut off the water and listened. It was a woman talking to her grandbaby.

"Oh my God," Tara shouted. "There's someone in the house." She dried her hands on the dishtowel, and grabbed her cell phone from the kitchen counter.

"Hush little baby, don't you cry. Grandma's gonna buy you a mocking bird . . ."

She slipped off her shoes, to avoid warning the intruder of her approach. She tiptoed down the hall. The only sound was her heart pounding. She stopped and listened.

"And if that mockingbird won't sing, Grandma's gonna buy you a diamond ring. Tara walked up to the bedroom door and stopped. She

took in a deep breath. Quickly, she turned her head and looked into the bedroom, and just as quickly, pulled her head back. No one was there. This time, she took a longer look.

From the kitchen she heard, *"And if that looking glass gets broke . . ."*

The singing continued, but no one was in the room. Tara entered the bedroom. The baby was asleep, and the room was empty. She walked back to the kitchen and listened to the rest of the song.

"Now, go to sleep my baby. Grandma needs to go watch her shows while you take a nice nap."

"Grandma, can you make me 'noogets?'" the child asked.

"Of course. When you wake up, Grandma will make you her special chicken nuggets. Just for you. Now you go to sleep."

Tara heard a kiss followed by, "I love you."

She recognized the voice. She knew it well.

She tried to figure out how sounds from the monitor next door had been transmitted to hers. And vice versa.

Very interesting, Tara thought. *This could be a very powerful discovery.*

Twenty-Four

Several weeks had passed. Tara kept the baby monitor on all the time, regardless if her grandchild was at her home or not. She researched baby monitors, and how it was possible to hear another person's conversation from a different home. But all the information about radio frequencies, megahertz, and wireless information just made her eyes glaze over. Most likely, because Francine had an extra monitor, they were both on the same frequency.

She worried she was being hacked by Francine. When the family was visiting, Tara made sure she kept the baby monitor on a different channel, hoping the other family could not listen in to what she said.

Some of the conversations she had overheard at Francine's home were astounding. Tara knew what she was doing was wrong, but her hatred towards them overrode her good sense of decency. Because of them, she now had to shop in consignment stores and outlets. No longer could she patronize high-end stores at the mall. These days, everything she purchased had to be on sale, or she did without. The Palmieri family destroyed her life, and she knew that one day, she'd be able to use this information to seek her revenge.

It wasn't long before she hit 'pay day.' The dialogue she overheard was one that would come in handy. She was sure of it. She was conniving. She was shrewd.

She grabbed her cell phone, placed it up against the monitor, and recorded the latest conversation. She didn't say anything to Carmine about what she heard, thinking maybe it was a prank. But the more she thought about it, the more she believed what she heard. And the more she liked the plan she had concocted.

Two days later, she told her husband, "Carmine, we need to talk."

"Now what?" he snapped. "I don't have any money to give you to buy that dress you saw in the window," he said with disgust.

"I'm not asking you for any money, you fool," she snapped back. "Besides, the only place I shop these days is at Goodwill, thanks to your greed."

"Are we going to go over that again? I just got home and you're going to nag me about something stupid? I'm in no mood."

Tara held her tongue for what she really wanted to tell her husband of thirty years. "What I have to say, you won't believe. We have to go into the bathroom to talk about this."

Carmine looked intrigued. "The bathroom? Are you serious?"

"Yes. I don't want our conversation overheard."

"Overheard by who? There's no one here except us. Are you going batty?"

"Shut up, and come with me."

Carmine followed her into the bathroom. She closed the door behind him. Tara took out her cell phone. "Listen to this," she said as she played the recording.

"Who's that talking?" her husband asked.

"Anthony and Vinny."

The hairs on the back of Carmine's neck rose. "I don't believe what I'm hearing. Those two kids are idiots, always playing pranks on people. Maybe they knew you were listening, and they said all this just to get you crazy."

"You're the idiot, Carmine. Listen to what they're saying. I missed the very beginning of their conversation, but hear what they're planning to do. What's interesting, is that Francine turns on the monitor when the grandkids are there, and that's what I usually hear. Sometimes I hear arguments between Francine and Johnny, too."

"You do? Why didn't you tell me about that? How long have you been listening in on their conversations?" Carmine asked.

"A few weeks."

"A few weeks," he shouted. "What the hell do you do all day? Sit around and listen in on my brother's life?"

"Don't you start with me," she snapped back. "The only time I hear anything is when their monitor is turned on. I'm telling you that what Anthony and Vinny are planning is real. I have a feeling Francine wanted to be nosy and listen in on her boys. Why else would she have turned on the monitor? You know she's a 'Helicopter Mother,' even though the boys are thirty.

"I don't like this, Tara. It ain't right. You need to mind your own business. What if they're listening in on our conversations?"

"I change the channel on the monitor whenever I have it on. Besides, I only turn it on when Veronica leaves the baby here," she lied.

"Well, I still don't like that you're eavesdropping," Carmine said. "Besides, why are you having me listen to this, anyway?"

Tara took her time before answering. "Because, we might be able to use this to get back at those bastards for making you suffer . . . for making our daughter suffer . . . for forcing you to take away what was rightly and legally yours. Now, we can get even with the Palmieri Family."

Get even with Johnny, thought Carmine.

Twenty-Five

Tara looked out her bay window before heading out for her morning jog. She needed to be sure no one from next door was out in their yard or in the driveway. Her husband left early in the morning, so he didn't have to worry about running into his brother, or his family. Instead, she was left playing the avoidance game that had been going on for years. She wished her husband would agree to move to another town and get away from this uncomfortable situation. But, Carmine was stubborn, like his brother and their father.

"Let him move first," Carmine yelled at Tara. "I ain't going nowhere."

They were surrounded by Palmieri family members, living next door and in the immediate area. They all knew about Carmine's indiscretions, and ostracized him, Tara, and their daughter Veronica and her family. She didn't care they didn't talk to her family any longer. His relatives were a bunch of nosey, opinionated gavones.

Tara saw the Palmieri front door open, so she stepped back into her house. She stood at the window and watched through the shear curtain.

Vinny, her entitled nephew, was leaving for work. She watched as he placed his coffee travel mug and work bag on top of the car. He took off his jacket, opened the back door on the driver's side, and placed the jacket on the hook above the window. He grabbed his thermos from the top of the car, leaned into the car, and Tara assumed, put the container into the cup holder.

Then he grabbed his work bag and tossed it in the front seat. Remaining on top of the car was a small brown note book that must have slipped out of his case. Vinny turned to answer his mother – the cow – who yelled something to her son. Vinny walked back and took a brown bag from his mother. "She probably made her baby boy his lunch," she mumbled to herself. She hated Johnny's family for what they did to her household. "Bastards. All of them," Tara said out loud.

Vinny got into his car, tossed the brown lunch bag over his shoulder into the backseat, and started up the car. He clipped on his seatbelt and quickly pulled out of the driveway. Tara was about to call after him that his notebook was still on top of his car, but she caught herself in time. *Whatever did he do for me,* she wondered? *He and his twin are nasty. It's obvious, the apple doesn't fall far from the tree,* she added. *Let the twit go looking for it later.* A bit of satisfaction ran through her as she stared at the notebook sitting on the blacktop.

Tara waited until nine o'clock to leave for her jog, when she knew her sister-in-law would be watching one of her TV court shows.

Then, she opened her front door, looked up and down the street, and started her slow jog. She stopped in front of the notebook, bent down and pretended to be tying her shoelace. Staying in a crouched position, she quickly picked it up and surreptitiously slipped it into the pocket of her Adidas jacket, and moved on quickly.

When she got home, she removed a cold Diet Coke from the refrigerator, and slinked into a wingchair in her family room. She opened the book and started reading.

Tentative Date: Tuesday, Aug. 27. Might move because of weather.

Sunset around 7:30.

Low tide 3 in afternoon.

High tide 9:30

Meet at sandbar at Silver Sands at 3.

Get J to the island by 4.

Steal 2 of mom's pills.

Buy waterproof case for phone.

Call A at work. FaceTime.

Go to island with A. Check out place first.

Bring crackers, cheese, box wine.

Tara read the shocking entries with great satisfaction. *Now,* she thought, *I have written proof of what I heard on the monitor.*

Twenty-Six

For the past year, Simone's life was one uncontrollable roller coaster, culminating with fighting for her life. Images that flashed through her mind caused panic attacks, night sweats, difficulty breathing, and exhaustion.

Simone recalled a session with her therapist days after defending her life.

"You have PTSD, Simone," her doctor told her. "You might have it for years. Understand it. Face your fears. Accept the memories. Don't fight them."

Simone was reminded of a poster she saw years ago in Greenwich Village: *FEAR–Forget Everything And Run, or, Face Everything And Rise. The Choice is Yours.*

"Sometimes I feel as if I'm reliving the nightmare over and over again."

Her therapist listened as Simone retold the story about the most recent horrific experience. "How do I make the nightmares go away?" She begged the doctor for a solution. "It took me years to get over Joe dying in my arms . . . and now . . ." her sentence trailed off.

"Simone, you've lived through several dramatic events, starting with your father raping you when you were twelve. Then the death of your parents, followed by Joe, and then the violence that took place in your home."

Simone wiped away tears as she recounted it all.

"Remember, when you feel as if you're in hell, keep on going.

You will get out to the other side. Are you writing in your gratitude journal?" the doctor asked. "You know that helped you in the past."

"Not as often as I should," Simone admitted. "I'll try to pick that up again. It really did help me see the wonderful things in my life, instead of only the negative."

The doctor continued. "Start writing about Charlie, and how happy you are with him in your life. He's brought you great joy."

"Yes, he has," she said, nodding. "He's wonderful."

"You're a strong woman, Simone. You've had to pick yourself up and start all over again several times in your life. You can get through this latest crisis. It will take time, but you'll find your inner strength again. Just understand that these experiences are in the past."

Simone left her therapist's office feeling renewed and determined.

That night she told Charlie, "I need to do an analysis of the past year. I must dig deep in order to understand all the events that occurred, ending in the demise of my stalker. My doctor suggested I pick up my gratitude journal again."

"That did help you in the past, my love," Charlie said.

"I'm so happy we're going to Paris in a few days. I'll have time to write, relax and maybe start the New Year off in a more positive direction." Simone mused, "The hardest part will be figuring out what happened between Jennifer and me, to understand what caused her to walk away from our business and our friendship. She knew about my stalker, and never told me she had information that could have changed the course of events."

Charlie said nothing, remembering how he was drugged and left for dead by this deranged person.

Simone and Charlie arrived on December twenty-fourth to a snow-covered Paris. Together, in a safe place, they would calmly recount all that had happened during that past year.

While they were in Paris, Simone's home in Connecticut was under construction to remove evidence resulting from the violence that had taken place. Once Pete, her contractor, notified her that it was safe to return to Westport and a newly renovated home, she and Charlie would book their tickets to the States.

Christmas Eve was celebrated in Simone's penthouse apartment, joined by everyone who was important to her: Mrs. Virginia Smith, her daughter Judy and her fiancé, Harold, and the Smith's housekeeper, Irene. Mr. Smith had had a five-bedroom penthouse apartment on Rue des Barres in Paris, France which he left to Simone in his will. He also willed his daughter, and Simone's best friend, Judy with a matching apartment across the hall.

After a meal of perfectly prepared local foods and several bottles of champagne, that rendered Irene tipsy, Charlie clicked his wine glass, and said he had an announcement to make. His divorce was finalized a few weeks before. He held up the papers and waved them over his head. Everyone cheered and drank to his release from Eve, a shrewd, conniving and manipulative woman. From the first day she had met Charlie, she had created a plan on how to get him to marry her . . . rather how she could marry the Hamilton money.

Eve told Charlie she was pregnant with his child, and forced him to marry her. If he didn't, she'd disgrace him to his family and to the community by saying he raped her. On their honeymoon, she allegedly had a miscarriage. For ten years Charlie believed she was trying to get pregnant. Then one day he found her birth control pills in a dresser drawer. Anger and rage consumed him. He had been played as a fool for years. He began divorce proceedings after Eve admitted she never wanted her perfect figure to be destroyed by carrying a child. She dragged out the divorce for years, making sure she was married to Charlie for a full ten years, so that in the future, she could collect his Social Security benefits. Charlie paid her handsomely, enough to force her to move away from the Hamilton estate and family.

Following his announcement of the divorce, Charlie then shocked the attendees with another announcement. He turned to Simone, got down on one knee, and presented her with a two carat diamond ring, asking her to be his wife. Jubilant cheers and congratulations followed after Simone said yes.

Simone was as surprised as everyone else at the table. She stared at the ring and began crying. This time, tears of joy and happiness. Left behind in Connecticut were the horrors of the past year.

"Can we get married in Paris, Charlie?" Simone asked after the shock wore off.

"Of course, my love. Anything you want."

"Will it be legal?" Irene asked in between her inebriated burps. "Oh, excuse me!"

Everyone laughed.

"Harold is a justice of the peace," Judy interjected. "He can perform a ceremony here, and then again in the States . . . just to make it legal," Judy said smiling at Irene.

On New Year's Eve, in front of the glittering and magnificent Eiffel Tower, Simone and Charlie exchanged vows and wedding bands, and became – unofficially – husband and wife.

"This was the easiest wedding I ever worked," Simone said, smiling at her husband.

Twenty-Seven

Once back in Connecticut, they planned a more formal ceremony and reception to be held at the Hamilton Grand Hotel, which Charlie's family owned. The wedding was scheduled for mid-April, when the forsythia, one of Simone's favorite flowers, would be in bloom. The guest list of forty people was small, compared to weddings Simone organized for hundreds of guests. In attendance were a few close friends, Charlie's family, Virginia and Judy Smith, and Irene, who was now Virginia's home-care aid.

It had been months since the surprise engagement, and their "test run wedding vows", a phrase the couple secretly called their wedding in front of the Eiffel Tower. Now, on one of the happiest days of her life, she still felt an emptiness in her heart.

Simone looked around at her guests. A lump formed in her throat. There was one special person missing from this glorious event, and that was Jennifer. She wished her friend and former business partner could have celebrated this day with her, but phone calls, texts and emails to Jennifer went unanswered and unreturned.

The next day Simone and Charlie headed out to the Hamptons for a mini honeymoon for three days. They booked a room in a bed and breakfast with an ocean view. Although it was still April, and the air was bone-chilling, they took long walks along the beach. They slept late, and found antiques in Sag Harbor to add to Simone's eclectic décor back in Westport.

"What is it, Simone?" Charlie asked as they stopped for hot chocolate in the village. "You've been very quiet today. Are you feeling okay?"

"My gut is telling me Jennifer is in danger. You know how I trust my instincts, and I can't ignore the reoccurring feelings that something just isn't right with her. I have to find out once and for all if she's safe."

Simone reached into her handbag, and retrieved her cell phone.

"Hi Marc," Simone said when she heard the man's strong voice on the other end of the phone. "It's Simone."

"Sim-Sim!" he cheered. "How are you? It's good to hear from you."

Marc Rosenzweig was a private investigator in New Jersey. Simone and Jennifer were the planners for numerous family events: his children's Mitzvahs, engagement parties, bridal showers, and most recently, his daughter's wedding attended by six hundred people. He and his wife had referred numerous friends, colleagues and family members to Simone. Work included small events, simple baby showers, and large weddings. These referrals resulted in substantial income to her company.

Over the past several years, Marc had investigated several people for Simone. When she suspected people surrounding Casey Bouvier, a bride who died hours before her wedding, he gathered significant information about each person. From his report she was able to conclude who was the one who killed Casey, although there were several people to suspect. It seemed each person investigated had good reason to murder Casey Bouvier, including the groom.

He asked, "How's life in Connecticut? How's Jennifer?"

"Well, that's why I'm calling you. I need help finding Jennifer."

"Is she missing?"

Simone proceeded to inform him about the events that happened over the past year, including details about her stalker, and the final results. She explained that she paid Jennifer to dissolve her interest in "I Do" and since then, hadn't been able to reach her. She worried that Jennifer was now in trouble.

"I understand, Simone. I'm sorry to hear about Jennifer. I'm sure she's fine. She's a smart woman. Don't worry. She's probably angry because you don't like her latest boyfriend."

Before saying goodbye, the two chatted about Charlie, his extensive family, and their mutual lives. Marc said he would look into finding Jennifer.

"Thanks, Marc. Love to Shelly and the kids."

Twenty-Eight

A week later, Simone heard her cell phone ringing while she was in the shower. She had missed a call from Marc. While she prepared her breakfast, she dialed his number.

"Hello, Marc. Sorry I wasn't able to talk when you called earlier. Have you found out anything?"

"Yes, I have, Simone. It's not good news, I'm afraid."

Simone braced herself for the worse. "Is she dead?"

"I don't think so. Let's say, I haven't found a death certificate with her name on it. Her mother hasn't heard from her for several weeks. She works for a company in Hartford as an Event Coordinator. Meager salary, compared to what she was making working with you."

"That doesn't sound so terrible. Is there more?"

"Yes, I'm afraid so. The man she lives with, Anthony Palmieri is a real piece of work. He was arrested for stealing a car when he was a teen. This was expunged because of his age. I've discovered a few other juvenile instances for him. He must have a twin, because a Vinny Palmieri with the same age at the same address showed up with a few juvie occurrences.

"Yes, I do remember Jennifer saying he had an identical twin."

"I think one of his parents paid off someone to remove these charges."

He continued his report. "Anthony and Jennifer own a home in Milford." He rattled off the address. "It's a modest home on the beach.

Mortgage payments and property taxes haven't been paid for over six months. They're about to lose the house."

"Do you know how much money they owe?" Simone asked, her mind racing.

"It's a little under $200,000 on the mortgage. I don't have the figures on the real estate taxes, but I can find out." He paused. "I know what you're thinking, Simone. Run it past Sidney, your attorney before you do anything. You might be trying to win a battle, but will lose the war in the end."

"Thanks Marc. I knew you'd come up with some juicy dirt."

"My pleasure, Sim-Sim. I'll send you a full report in the mail. Let me know if there's anything else I can do for you."

Simone's next call was to her attorney, Sidney Harding.

"Hi Sid. It's Simone. I need your help creating a new LLC. And I need for my name to be buried, without any trace back to me." She proceeded to explain her idea and plans.

"I'll see what I can do," Sid said. "You're a woman who never ceases to surprise me."

Twenty-Nine

On Tuesday morning, August twenty-seventh, Anthony said he didn't need to get to work until ten o'clock, so he was going to get an extra hour of sleep.

"I'll see you later at Silver Sands," he told Jennifer, as she gave him a quick kiss on the head.

As soon as Anthony heard Jennifer's car pull out of the driveway, he jumped out of bed. He needed to carry out the next step of his plan, and still get to work on time.

He dragged a matching set of luggage out of the attic, and filled them with Jennifer's possessions: clothes, shoes, makeup, and anything else he could find, and shoved it all into the three suitcases. What didn't fit, he put in garbage bags. He put the stuffed suitcases back up in the attic, the contents to be disposed of slowly over the next few months.

He pulled the envelope out from under the mattress, re-reading the letter inside. Before he walked out the door, he left the envelope in plain sight on the kitchen table, where his mother would find it first.

He didn't say good-bye to Goober. He just walked out the door, and headed to work as if it was any other day of the week.

Thirty

At noon, on Tuesday, August twenty-seventh, Francine got in her car and headed to Anthony's cottage. She'd tidy up, walk Goober, and snoop. Upon arrival, she noticed something was different. First, Goober didn't want to come out of his crate. He whimpered, and refused treats offered to him.

"What's the matter, Goober? I never thought I'd say this, but you look sad." *Was it possible for a dog to look depressed?* Francine wondered.

She left his crate open, and went into the kitchen. The sink was free of dishes, and the counter was cleaned off. She headed upstairs to get a load of wash. She was about to remove items from the closet hamper when she stopped short. All the rows of Jennifer's outfits and shoes were gone. The only remaining clothes belonged to Anthony.

Immediately, she began to snoop. She browsed the dressers. Jennifer's garments were gone: her jewelry, handbags, and toiletries from the bathroom had disappeared.

Francine went back downstairs and looked around for some tell-tale sign of her possessions. Knickknacks that Jennifer had brought with her from her apartment were no longer in the bookcases.

She went back into the kitchen, and looked around. On the table, nestled between the napkin holder and the salt and pepper shakers, was an envelope with Anthony's name typed on the front. The envelope wasn't sealed. Francine opened the envelope and read the typed letter.

Anthony, I've left you for someone else. Things between us haven't been good for a few months. You come home late, you party all the time, and you refuse to set a wedding date. So I've decided to move on. Jennifer

---

Francine sat down and began laughing. Hysterical guffaws echoed throughout the house. Goober's curiosity got the best of him, and he trotted into the kitchen. He put his head on Francine's lap and looked up at with pitiful eyes.

That's why you're so sad, Goober. Your bitch left you. Well, ain't that a wonderful thing. Anthony is finally free to find himself a nice Italian girl, who will fatten you up with meatballs and braciole. This is wonderful, Goober." She rubbed the dog's head. He let out a yawn, and headed back to his crate.

"Oh no, you don't," Francine said. "You're going out for a walk. And we're getting ice cream to celebrate."

Before leaving, she went back in the kitchen, folded up the note, and placed it back in the envelope.

"A wonderful day it is," Francine said cheerfully.

As she and Goober walked the neighborhood, Francine didn't give a second thought that today was the day her sons were taking Jennifer to Charles Island, leaving her there to die. She assumed Jennifer must have overheard the twins talking, and decided to leave town beforehand. *Maybe she's not as stupid as I thought.*

Thirty-One

On Tuesday, August twenty-seventh, Jennifer arrived at Silver Sands at two o'clock, when she'd meet Mary Ann at the entrance to the boardwalk. There, they'd chat for a while before Jennifer met Anthony. She stopped at the rock cemetery, as she fondly called the vast display of cairns. The area, no more than fifty feet wide, looked like a place of rest, the rocks standing like markers for the graves of tiny sea creatures. Today, many of them were toppled over, either by rambunctious kids, birds landing on them, or angry tides.

"Hi Jennifer," Mary Ann said as she approached the bench, distracting Jennifer from her thoughts. Her friend was wearing her signature floppy hat and sunglasses, dressed in white linen shorts and a light blue tank top.

Jennifer wore a bikini under a silk cover up, and her red Keds tied tightly so her feet would be secured for the trek to Charles Island. Her feet craved the preferred familiar angles associated with wearing spike high heels.

After their walk, Jennifer asked Mary Ann, "Why don't you hang around and wait for Anthony. I'd like for you to meet him."

"I'd like to," she said, "but maybe another time. I've got a dinner tonight and I need to get back home. Hopefully, I'll see you next week."

The women said their goodbyes. Mary Ann turned and walked back to her car, and Jennifer headed toward the warning signs at the foot of the tombolo. It was sad to think that in a few weeks the water will be too cold, the ground too hard, and the leaves on the island gone, stripping away their hideaway. She had to admit, she enjoyed Anthony's new-found lovemaking spot on Charles Island. Their relationship seemed to be stronger since she had threatened to leave him and move back to her apartment. But, their "sexcapades" would have to wait until next year. Hopefully by then, she would be Mrs. Anthony Palmieri.

Her thoughts turned to Anthony's promises of marriage, and how every time she brought up the subject, he found a way to create an excuse. He wanted to save enough money so that when she did get pregnant, they would not have to worry about finances. He also needed his car fixed for $3,000. She thought back to that day; she hadn't heard any knocking from the engine the night before, but suddenly, on his way to work, Anthony had to have the car towed to the shop, where it stayed for three days.

So he said . . .

Jennifer stood looking out at Charles Island. She paid close attention to the tide, which then appeared unusually higher, causing some concern. Anthony told her the tide wasn't coming in until seven that evening, four hours away. Her thoughts were interrupted by a kiss on her neck.

"Hi Jennifer," came the voice from behind her.

She swung her body around and looked up at Anthony towering over her, now six inches shorter without her high heels.

"Whatcha thinking about?" he asked.

"You," she lied. And realized this was one of the rare times he called her by her name.

He wore Bermuda shorts, a tight fitting light blue tank top, a baseball cap, and dark polarized sunglasses. On his back he carried a lightweight backpack containing a blanket, two individual wine boxes, and snacks.

"Ready to go?" he asked.

"Did you check the tides, Anthony? The water seems higher than usual, given that the tide doesn't come in for another four hours."

"Yeah, it does look a little high, but maybe there's a tanker out there that caused some big wakes." *She's such a dumbass, she'll believe me,* he thought to himself.

"Good point. Okay, I'm ready," Jennifer said, smiling up at him.

There was a scattering of sunbathers. Many families left early to get the children out of the sun. A group of kids dug in the mud for tiny sea creatures, made mud pies they quickly squashed, or were splashed by the incoming waves.

They walked single file along the tombolo, being cautious not to slip between the boulders, getting a foot stuck, or worse, a leg. The boulders were covered with slime from seaweed and beach grass. Gingerly and with extreme caution they made their way along the half-mile hike to Charles Island.

"You smell differently today," she said after they had reached their destination.

His mind, racing for an answer said, "I tried a new soap this morning," he said.

"I didn't see a new soap in the bathroom." For an instant, her mind listed reasons, one being he had had sex with another woman, and he showered at her home.

"I didn't like the smell, so I threw it out," he responded quickly.

Jennifer took Anthony's hand in hers, and noticed it was smoother than in the past. "Your hand is softer than usual."

"I've been moisturizing. Gotta keeps things lubricated, if you know what I mean," he said with a sly grin. "How about you lead the way," he said trying to change the subject.

They walked around to the back of the island, and squeezed their bodies through the cut chicken wire. They settled near the remnants of an old brick building with a collapsed fire pit. From the backpack they removed the blanket, the wine and snacks. They indulged in the meager nibbles of a few crackers and chunks of cheddar cheese. "Why did you get cheddar?" Jennifer asked. "You know that's my least favorite."

"I was in a rush. Sorry." *The minor details were beginning to surface . . . his body smell and feel . . . the food . . . what else,* he wondered.

"That's okay. Can I have some wine?"

Small Black Box wines were consumed straight from the cartons. She, pinot grigio. He, cabernet.

After Jennifer took three slips of wine, she said she was already feeling its effects.

"You didn't have much to eat, maybe that's why," he said. "Finish your wine before it spills."

Jennifer lifted the half empty box and drained its contents.

She smiled at him, and he took advantage of her vulnerability. He helped her remove her cover-up dress. His excitement was building quickly. He groped at her bikini, kissing her with renewed passion. He was ravenous. He barely got out of his Bermuda shorts, his excitement growing exponentially. "You turn me on," he said as he rushed to enter her.

Jennifer was surprised by Anthony's excitement. Was it the excitement of being caught, or was it her sense that he was acting differently. If there was anything Jennifer learned from Simone, it was to trust your inner voice. "Your gut speaks louder than your tongue," she often told Jennifer.

Today, Jennifer was once again recalling these words of wisdom. There was something different about Anthony. Subtle differences: he was more attentive, he spoke with a gentler voice, his skin was softer, and he smelled differently. He had called her by her name. She decided she was being overly paranoid, and anxious about wanting to have "the talk" with him later tonight about setting a wedding date.

He had left his sunglasses on during the walk to the island, so she couldn't see if he had engaged in some illegal activity before meeting her. She found a roach-clip on the patio table last week, and recently had been smelling pot. He said it belonged one of his poker buddies.

Her vision blurred, and her mind was becoming muddled, thick with thoughts that she couldn't decipher.

Their lovemaking ended as quickly as it had started. He rolled off her. She was suddenly feeling very sleepy. She could hardly keep her eyes opened. Trees appeared distorted as a bout of vertigo loomed. What was happening? She tried sitting up, but it was difficult to lift her head. She reached for Anthony, who was now standing up. He was naked, and had his back to her.

"I don't feel well," she mumbled.

She watched as he bent over to pick up his bathing shorts.

"Anthony," she said. "Where's your tattoo?"

Anthony turned and looked at her, confused. "Tattoo?"

Something strange was happening to her. "Anthony?"

No answer.

All her senses came together at once, and she realized she wasn't on the island with Anthony. "Vinny. Is that you?" was all she could utter before darkness took over.

Vinny looked down at Jennifer. Her statement surprised him. *Does Anthony have a tattoo I don't know about?*

He quickly went through the final motions of the plan. He poured out the rest of his wine container, which was filled with grape juice. Then he rolled Jennifer over onto the ground and pulled the blanket out from under her. He took her bathing suit, cover-up, the blanket, and shoved it all into the backpack. He was about to close the bag when he looked back at Jennifer's naked body. A sudden wave of guilt soared through him. He removed her cover-up dress from the backpack, and tossed it near her body. He pulled out his cell phone, encased in a waterproof case and called his brother.

"Hey bro, it's done. No problems."

"Good," Anthony responded back. Then Vinny hit the FaceTime icon.

"Hey everybody, Vinny's on the phone," Anthony shouted to Felix and the other guys around him. They yelled back their hellos.

"Hey Vin, where are you?"

"I'm still at work. I'll be here until around five-thirty, six."

Anthony asked, "Want to meet me at Stonebridge for drinks?" Anthony turned around and asked his co-workers if they wanted to join in.

Felix walked up to Anthony and looked at his phone. There was his mirror image. "Man, you two really do look alike."

"Can you join us, Felix?" came the face on Anthony's phone.

"Yeah, sure," he said with a hesitation. He became silent for a moment and stared at Vinny's face. *That's strange, when did the gas station get trees?* Felix wondered. *And when was Vinny allowed to go to work with a tank top on?*

The brothers ended their call. Anthony went back to doing his work, while Felix wondered why something about that conversation had confused him. He decided not to say anything to Anthony. *No good reason to get nosy about my friend's brother.*

Vinny zipped up the backpack and placed it on his shoulders. He looked around one last time before he headed off the island. The sun was quickly setting, the air was getting cooler, and the tide was moving in faster than expected. His timing had been off. If he hadn't had his way with Jennifer, he would have been off the island by now. *Had Anthony told me incorrect tide times?*

Vinny knew the undertow and currents were extremely dangerous, and hoped he'd be able to make it back to land. He looked around and quickly decided on the best place to start his trek back to the mainland.

The boys had grown up on the water. His parents owned a sailboat, and the twins were high school lifeguards during the summer. They were strong swimmers. Both had participated a few times, along with the police authorities on rescues from Charles Island. He knew the dangers he faced, and that he'd have to muster up all his energy and strength.

He suddenly realized he could never swim back to shore with the backpack pulling him down. He removed it, and turned back towards Jennifer's sleeping body. He found some bricks near the fire pit, and buried the pack as best as he could. He covered it up with brush, and a few large rocks. He'd have to come back for it another time, unless it got washed out to sea. Along with Jennifer's body. He put his cell in his back pocket, and buttoned it closed.

Vinny got a quarter of the way back to shore on the tombolo, when a wave knocked him into the water. He struggled to come up for air as another wave crashed over his head, momentarily blinding him, and causing him to lose his bearings. He turned around and saw the island ahead, and knew he had to turn around again. He remembered an important fact: *swim parallel to the land to avoid the undertow.*

He used all his strength and swimming acumen to fight the current. He was a strong swimmer, but it was still difficult to fight the tide. He was almost at the shore when another incoming wave pulled him down. He focused on trying to float. Relax, he told himself. Vinny resurfaced, and started swimming again. His muscles burned, but he was determined not to give up. *I must survive.*

He surfaced on a private beach, a quarter mile from where his journey had originated. He collapsed on the sand, exhausted, and panting for air. His chest ached. He had used every ounce of strength and stamina. His legs protested at his attempts to stand up and walk. He had to get to Stonebridge to meet his brother, but he was drained and exhausted. He rested for a few minutes. Sand stuck to his wet, cold body and he began shivering. His saliva was salty, his eyes teared and his ears hummed.

Vinny mustered up all of his energy, and stood up. His body shook from the cold air against his wet body. His teeth chattered. He walked the distance back to his car, rubbing his arms and legs, trying to keep warm.

He was two blocks from where he left his car, but it could have been a mile away. The walk was arduous. He stumbled and cursed when his bare foot stepped on a broken seashell. He continued to run his hands vigorously up and down his arms in order to maintain some body heat.

Finally, he reached his car. He ran his hand along the back tire until he found the key he had placed there. He opened the trunk, grabbed a towel, and wrapped it around his body. He started the car, and put the heater on full blast. While the car and his body warmed up, he took several long swigs of Gatorade, replenishing his lost energy. Once his body warmed, he slipped into the backseat. He twisted and turned until he got out of his wet bathing suit. He dried off. Then, he got back into his casual outfit of jeans and a polo shirt. He returned to the front seat, looked at himself in the vanity mirror, ran his fingers through his damp hair, and smiled sinisterly. *Yeah, I can see what Ant sees in her. She has — had — a rocking body.*

Before he pulled out of the parking lot, he glanced once more over at Charles Island. It had become true to its name - an island.

It wouldn't be until four in the morning before low tide, when Jennifer could find her way back to the beach. That is, if she had survived the night.

Another wave of guilt passed through him, but quickly dissipated when he considered the money he and Anthony were about to inherit.

He left the parking lot and headed to Stonebridge Restaurant. The further he got from the beach, the better he began feeling. Tomorrow, his muscles would remind him of the brilliantly planned scenario, and his incredible physical strength.

Vinny walked into Stonebridge, refreshed from the Gatorade, relieved that the job was completed. He was thirsty for some celebratory beer.

"Hi Felix," he said.

Felix looked at him with confusion. *Was he wearing different clothes than before?* "Hi," he said casually.

Vinny saddled up to the bar. "A Bud, please," he told the bartender.

Anthony asked in a whisper, "Did anyone see you?"

Vinny shook his head. The two clinked glass bottles. "Here's to being rich," Anthony whispered.

Felix, who sat across the way from the twins thought, *They think I'm a jerk, but something's going on with those two. I don't know what, but they're up to something.*

No one had seen Vinny, other than the woman sitting under the beach umbrella, taking photos of the happy couple walking out to Charles Island with her telephoto lens.

Thirty-Two

On Tuesday August twenty-seventh, Tara returned home from the beach at five o'clock. She paced the floors in her house. She walked from the kitchen to the bedroom, to the basement, back up to the kitchen. "What should I do?" she kept asking herself. She went for a walk around the neighborhood, but the endorphins did nothing to calm her anxiety.

Vinny took Jennifer out to Charles Island, and was going to leave her there for dead.

She thought about calling Carmine, but he was at work, then going to play in a softball game. He told her to mind her own business when she told him about the conversation she overhead. Maybe she should call the Coast Guard, but what would she tell them? She considered the parish priest, but quickly dismissed that idea.

Tara looked outside. It was getting dark. If Jennifer hadn't gotten off the island, she'll be there until the next low tide. Looking on her cell, Tara checked the local tides. The next low tide wasn't until early the next morning. She decided she had to do something.

Tara got in her car and drove to the local 7-11 and purchased a disposable phone. She only needed to make one phone call. She hoped the call couldn't be traced.

She drove to Ansonia, the valley section of Connecticut. She placed a wad of tissues over the phone's mouthpiece.

"Hello, Milford Police. How may I help you?"

"I want to report an attempted murder of a young woman."

"May I have your name, please?"

"No . . . no names. Someone was left for dead on Charles Island."

"And how do you know this?" asked the operator at the police station.

"I just know. I have evidence. The boyfriend did it. Please, send help."

Tara hung up, then tossed the phone into the river.

Thirty-Three

On Charles Island the cold air attacked Jennifer's naked body. All she had on were her red Keds. She awoke in complete darkness, shivering, and disoriented. Her head pounded. She tried to sit up, but a wave of nausea made her vomit. She looked around for Anthony . . . no . . . Vinny. It was Vinny who brought her out to the island, she was sure of it. But why? Why was she abandoned on Charles Island? She searched for an answer.

She wrapped her arms around her chest, trying to warm up. She tried focusing on her surroundings, but it was too dark to see anything. Her hands groped for her belongings. The only thing she felt were the ground, twigs, and leaves. She got onto her knees and tried to feel her way, trying to remember where she was on the island. Her hand stopped at something silky - her cover-up. She quickly put it on and immediately felt comforted having something next to her skin.

She must have slept for a long time. She remembered they arrived on the island close to sunset. Now, the sky was pitch black and the stars were out. She tried organizing her thoughts through the brain fog.

Fortunately for her, the moon was almost full, and she could see shadows cast along the path. She heard the waves crashing nearby. The tide was in. Could she get off the island? She wasn't a good swimmer, and she would never survive. Besides, there wasn't any trace of the tombolo. It was completely immersed with water.

She attempted to stand up, but her head swirled, and her ears buzzed. She rolled onto her knees, and her calves began to cramp. Trying to move her legs resulted in scraped knees. She hung her head, hoping to stop the vertigo. Very slowly, Jennifer stood up, and grabbed onto a branch to balance herself. She was cold and frightened.

Suddenly, she heard footsteps. She stopped walking and listened. Leaves rustled and twigs snapped. Footsteps mixed with crashing waves. *Was Vinny still on the island? Had he planned to kill her and push her body out to sea?* The footsteps were getting closer. She had to hide. But where? She couldn't see more than two feet in front of her, and there weren't any hiding places.

As quietly as possible, Jennifer hid behind the largest tree she could find. Her head spun, her stomach churned. With all her might she willed herself not to throw up. But now, a fresh surge of fear ran through her. *What if he finds me?* She didn't have the strength to fight him off. Violent images flashed through her mind.

Did Anthony know that Vinny brought me out to Charles Island? How did Vinny know that Anthony and I came out here? Anthony must be involved in this scheme, Jennifer decided. She had to focus and prepare for fighting off Vinny, or whoever else was on the deserted island.

Jennifer's eyes welled up. *Why would Anthony and Vinny do this to me?* She reflected back on the last seven months. She and Anthony had purchased a home together, soon they'd be married, and they each purchased life insurance policies. Life insurance . . . suddenly, the scheme came together. *Anthony was going to claim the money on my life insurance policy. The house is in both our names, and he was her sole beneficiary. He's the Executor to my will. I'm so stupid.*

The reality of her mistakes came flooding back. She felt as if a dark curtain was lifted, and she could suddenly look at her life with renewed clarity and with a new direction.

Leaves rustled a yard from where she hid. Then there was silence. Waves continued to crash against the island.

Jennifer slowly moved her head from around the tree and came face to face with a pair of large brown eyes.

Thirty-Four

Jennifer's fear escalated when she stared into the curious eyes of a large buck. The two gawked at each other, equally startled, frightened, and shocked to find the other on the island. *How did a deer get on the island,* she wondered.

She considered petting the animal, but as she reached out to touch him, he snorted hot breath and bolted off. "Wait," she called after him. He was a comfort, she realized, another breathing, warm-blooded being, another heartbeat. But, he was gone.

A couple of years ago, a killer had held a gun to her head. That level of fear had returned. Her brain was muddled, her body shivered from the late-August night, and spasms of pain surged through her stomach. Only mosquitoes, gnats and ticks found warmth and food on her body.

She decided she needed to find the opening in the chicken wire, and make her way back to the tombolo. The first step away from the tree, brought renewed cramps in her calves and feet, but she persevered. She climbed over tree roots, downed trees and old bricks and stones. Shells cracked under her feet, and dug through her canvas shoes. She tripped again, this time on a red cross, an obvious burial spot. A powerful odor of dead mussels sent a wave of queasiness, and forced her to turn her head in the opposite direction of the smell.

Her arms, legs and torso were being pricked by overgrown bramble bushes and branches. She tripped over a tree root, and landed hard on her knees and palms. Her cover-up got snagged on a branch and tore.

Nausea took hold again, and she had to stop. Stomach spasms made her cry out in pain. She regained her balance, and again began her slow trek. Her knees and legs were bleeding from falling onto sweetgum pods. Charles Island was only fourteen acres, but it could have been a hundred as far as she was concerned. The spirits of Indians and other legendary ghosts that inhabited the island seemed to walk with her, whispering their support and comfort. *You can do it.*

"Help!" she screamed at the top of her lungs into the darkness. She screamed again. No response, other than the sound of waves, and occasional rustling of the trees. It would be hours before she could get off the island. She climbed over boulders and through the densely forested land. She fell again, and this time, she screamed from the pain in her ankle. She tried standing up, but the searing pain caused her to fall, and introduced a new wave of panic.

Her thoughts turned to Simone, and how she would transform into a strong, determined woman, ready to take on the world in time of danger and conflict. Jennifer learned from the best – it was time she applied what she was taught from the master.

"Simone," she yelled. "Help me!"

Slowly, Jennifer lifted herself up, and through cuts, scratches, dizzy spells, and possibly a broken ankle, she continued on.

Her ankle throbbed and swelled with each step. She stopped again as a fresh wave of pain gripped her body. Acid-tasting spittle dripped from her mouth. She stumbled again, this time she grabbed on to a tree to prevent another fall.

"Help," she screamed again, and again, until her throat was sore.

"Hello?" she heard in return. "Is someone there?"

"Help me. Please, someone help me," she begged. In the distance she saw a beam of light moving from left to right. The movement from the flashlight caused her equilibrium to give out. She leaned against a tree.

A man's voice commanded, "Keep talking, so we can find you."

But she couldn't speak through the fire inside her throat.

"We're coming to get you. Are you hurt?"

"Yes. Please, help me," she managed to whisper. "Yes."

Jennifer cried as fresh pain and weakness jolted through her body. She lifted her head, took a step, and slammed down onto the ground, hitting her head on a tree root.

Thirty-Five

Jennifer opened her eyes, but the bright lights forced them shut. She squinted until her pupils adjusted to the blinding stream of light. The room spun. Her head pounded. Her ankle throbbed. She shut her eyes again. She needed the pain to end, so she could think.

Where am I, and why is it so bright, she wondered. Even with her eyes closed she felt the heat of the lights on her face. She opened her eyes again. She focused on a stationary object to prevent the dizzy spell. She recalled being taught this trick while taking ice skating lessons. But the pain in her head wouldn't subside.

Jennifer suddenly realized her head was held in place by a brace. She moved her eyes slowly around the room. At the first hint of vertigo, she shut them. When she looked again, she took stock of her surroundings. Straps kept her tied to a bed. Beeps resounded, as well as a distant alarm. She heard voices, some soft, others filled with urgency. There were needles in her veins, attached to tall metal stands with hanging bags filled with various colored liquids.

Suddenly, the memories came flooding back. She was on Charles Island, barely dressed, and screaming for help. She remembered the cold air, deep brown eyes so close to hers, the beam of a flashlight.

"Hello," came a soft voice from the foot of the bed. "I'm Nurse Stephanie. You've got a nasty bump on your head, young lady."

"Hello." The word was barely audible, not much more than a whisper. Her throat was parched and sore. "Water," she said to the nurse.

"Soon, but not right now," she replied.

The nurse was dressed in white cotton pants, Dansko white clogs, and a Care Bear scrub top. Around her neck hung a lanyard with a credentials tag, and a koala bear clipped to the strap. Standing no more than five feet tall, her striking black eyes gave her a commanding appearance.

"How did I get here? My head hurts."

Nurse Stephanie said, "The Coast Guard found you, and brought you here. Someone made an anonymous call to the police, and they notified the water patrol. You were unconscious with a nasty head wound. The headache is from a concussion."

"What's wrong with my neck?" Jennifer whispered.

"The brace is to help keep you stable. You weren't a very patient patient," Stephanie said humorously. "Do you remember anything?"

"Not much," followed by a raspy, "Can't talk."

"You have to rest now. I'll be back in fifteen minutes to check on you. Meanwhile, close your eyes and try to sleep. I'll be back with the doctor."

As promised, the nurse returned with the doctor, who introduced himself as Dr. Brady. He was dressed casually in slim jeans, a tight fitting oxford shirt that complimented his eyes, and wore a stethoscope around his neck. Jennifer tried to remember his name, but it quickly escaped her memory.

"Well, who do we have here?" he asked as he began examining Jennifer. "Do you know your name?"

She nodded.

"Would you like to share it with me? After all, I don't usually examine a beautiful young woman without at least knowing her name first."

She smiled and thought, *Smooth. Very smooth.*

He repeated his question. "Do you know your name?"

She nodded again. Followed by, "Thirsty."

He checked the chart, examined Jennifer's throat, and agreed the patient could be given a few ounces of water.

"Thank you," she said after taking several sips.

"Slowly, please. I don't want you barfing on my vintage jeans," he teased.

Jennifer smiled again, and stared into his eyes. They matched hers.

"So, what do I have to do for you to tell me who you are?"

This time, Jennifer shook her head no. "I'm not telling you."

"Oh, so you want to be coy?" he teased again. "Or, do you have amnesia?"

"No, I don't have amnesia," she whispered. "I know my name, but I don't want him to know I'm alive."

This statement stopped the doctor's teasing. A serious, concerned look crossed his face. "Are you running from domestic abuse?"

"He left me on the island to die." These words brought forth a fresh round of tears. "Ow. My head . . . my head," she screamed as fresh pain stabbed at her brain.

The doctor sat down on her bed, placed his hands on either side of her, and said softly, "Okay, no more questions that will upset you. I'll come back later and we can chat again. Are you hungry?"

Jennifer sniffled, and nodded. The nurse handed her a wad of tissues.

"Don't blow too hard," the doctor instructed.

"Yes, I'm hungry, and very thirsty. I haven't eaten since yesterday morning . . . no, yesterday afternoon. I had some cheese and crackers. But I vomited on the island," Jennifer said. Then she remembered, "I had wine, but I think there was something in it because it made me fall asleep."

The doctor remained quiet for a few moments. "Well, I don't know how to tell you this, young lady, but you've been here for three days. You were found very late Tuesday night, close to midnight. We don't know how long you were out there. You're pretty beat up with cuts and bruises. You haven't had any solid food in days; you're being fed intravenously for now."

Jennifer stared at his engaging eyes. "Oh."

"Would you like a big fat juicy hamburger?" he asked her, grinning, and lighting up his eyes.

Jennifer smiled.

"I'm teasing, sorry. I don't think your tummy is ready for something that heavy. But I will order up something enticing, like consume soup and Jell-O."

Jennifer stuck out her tongue with a 'blah' expression.

A fresh wave of leg pain made Jennifer yell, "My legs . . . my legs . . . cramps."

The nurse and the doctor immediately went to work massaging her legs. When the doctor touched her ankle, she cried out in pain. "That hurts a lot."

Dr. Brady looked at her chart, and read the notation that an x-ray of the ankle, upon admission, showed it was broken. He read the report out loud to Jennifer.

"I'll get some ice for her foot, doctor," the nurse said, and left him alone with Jennifer.

He smiled at her again.

He's got a great bedside manner. And gorgeous eyes.

"I noticed you were not wearing a wedding band. Are you single?"

"Are you asking me out?" she asked. Then quickly added, "Sorry, I didn't mean to say that."

He laughed. "I apologize. I'm just trying to learn if we need to call a spouse about your whereabouts, or if we need someone arrested for physical harm to you."

"If I tell you my name, will you keep it out of the press, and the TV?

As I said, I don't want him to know I'm alive."

"Well, I hate to burst your bubble, 'Miss-I-won't-tell-you-my-name', but you've been on the news since you've been found. The media has been banging on our door trying to get a statement. There's a policeman stationed outside your room for protection. So you see, we do need to know your name to confirm the media's information."

Jennifer remained silent for a few moments.

"And, there's more," said the doctor. "Someone took a photograph of you with a man walking out to Charles Island. The photo was released this afternoon, and the police have already made an arrest. Do you know an Anthony Palmieri?"

"Oh, my God," Jennifer said as another round of spontaneous tears took over.

"Is he the one who took you to Charles Island?"

Jennifer shook her head. "It was Vinny, I'm sure of it. His twin brother. He didn't have a tattoo."

The doctor looked quizzically up to the nurse. He instructed her to tell the police officer standing guard to be aware of a twin.

When the door closed, Jennifer looked up at the doctor and confessed, "My name is Jennifer Keys. I live . . . lived with Anthony Palmieri. It was his brother that took me out to Charles Island, pretending to be his twin." Between the tears she asked, "Why would they do this to me?" Panic ensued. "Oh please, please, don't let him know I'm alive. He'll figure out a way to kill me so he won't get charged. Please, keep this to yourself."

The doctor nodded, and promised he'd keep her identity a secret as long as legally possible. Then he asked, "Is there anyone we can call? Now that you're awake, and coherent, you might be released in two or three days. Since you've told me that your boyfriend and his brother are the ones who tried to kill you, you'll need another place to live. Is there anyone with whom you can stay?"

Jennifer thought for a long moment, then said, "Yes, there is. She's a friend, who lives near the beach. I don't have her phone number. I don't know where my cell phone is."

"You came in dressed in a cover-up and sneakers. That's all."

"If I give you her name, can you call her? I don't know her number, but I'm sure you can Google her."

Jennifer shared the information with the doctor. He punched numbers into his iPhone, and quickly found a contact number.

Thirty-Six

Text messages flew back and forth between Anthony and Vinny.

Anthony: *Shit, they found her. She's alive.*

Vinny: *Where is she?*

Anthony: *I don't know. The news said she's being held in an undisclosed location. We have to find her and shut her up. Start calling hospitals. Maybe call in some chips.*

Vinny: *You mean, get her knocked off?*

Anthony: *I have to think.*

Vinny: *I heard someone had evidence. What do we do?*

Anthony: *Get mom to vouch for you. She'll tell the cops you were home all day.*

Vinny: *She'll own my manhood.*

Anthony: *Do you have a choice?*

Vinny: *Put on Channel 12. My picture is there.*

Anthony turned on his TV. *Someone took a picture of you walking with her to the island?*

Vinny: *I didn't see no one. What are we going to do?*

Anthony: *Play it cool. I was at work. You called me from your job. Ma will vouch for you. The guys at work will say you were at work. Deny that's you.*

"Vincent Michael, come upstairs right now," came the booming voice from the kitchen.

Vinny: *Ant, ma just called me to go upstairs. I think she's watching the news.*

Vinny went to the kitchen. "Yeah, ma, what's up?"

"Sit down." Vinny had never seen his mother looking so pale, or as angry. "Is that you on the TV?" she said as she pointed to the screen. She recorded the news on her DVR and kept playing it over and over.

"Me?" he answered, squinting at the TV for added affect. "Why would you say that's me? That doesn't even look like me," he said playing dumb.

"Vincent Michael, stop it. I know what you did," his mother said in a tone he hadn't heard since he was a teenager. "That's you, and that's Jennifer. I know you and Anthony concocted a way to get her out to Charles Island."

Vinny's mouth dropped open. "I don't know what you're talking about," he lied. His mind raced, his heart beat faster while sweat formed on his upper lip. He was right: she *had* listened on the baby monitor the day he and Anthony discussed the plan.

"Now, I'm willing to forget this incident," Francine said.

"Forget this incident? There's nothing to forget," he said defensively. "There wasn't any incident. That's not me."

She gave him a warning look. "I'm not stupid. I heard you two in the basement. I didn't say anything because I thought you were playing a prank on me. You know I listen to everything that goes on in the basement."

Francine continued. "If the police ask, I'll tell them you were home all day with me, but you'll have to do something for me in return."

"But ma, it wasn't me," he kept up the pretense.

"Stop it, Vincent!" she shouted.

She's serious. Vinny knew he was trapped, and won't get out of this one.

"What do you want me to do?" he said, defeated. He still didn't admit to the crime. He knew if he did, his mother would hold it over him for the rest of their lives.

"I want you to marry Angie, and give me grandchildren right away."

"What?" Vinny couldn't believe what he was hearing. He got up to walk away.

"Sit down," she commanded.

He turned and shouted, "So, if I marry her, you'll lie to the police for me? You'll tell them I was home all day with you?"

There, he admitted to the crime, Francine acknowledged.

She continued, "Yes Vinny, I'll lie for you." Francine knew what she wanted most in her life, and who was going to give it to her. Johnny got her away from the Bronx and bought her a nice house in Connecticut. And now her son, too, is going to give her what she wants -- that her son marries a nice Italian girl and gives her more grandchildren.

"What about Ant?" he asked.

"I'll deal with him in my own way."

Thirty-Seven

On Wednesday evening, August twenty-eighth, Francine called a family meeting with the twins.

"Listen to me," she commanded. "This is how we are going to handle this situation. Vinny, you're going to say you went to work that day, but came home at two-thirty to help me in the garden. Then, you took me food shopping, and helped me with the groceries. Your father was working late. I'll vouch that you were with me in the afternoon, until you left for Stonebridge. Then, when the cops . . ."

"No, Ma. Too many lies, too many legs," Anthony interrupted. "I don't want you to say Vinny was here with you. I have a better idea."

Francine glared at him. "Well, Mr. Smarty-pants, tell me what *you're* thinking."

A combination of anger and mounting fear stirred inside Anthony. He could not believe his mother would demand that Vinny marry Angie in exchange for lying to the police. He lashed out. "On second thought, it's none of your business. Vinny and I will figure it out. If the cops ask you any questions, tell them you don't remember. Tell them you're a senile old woman. I don't care what you say. Just stay out of it."

Vinny stared at his brother in disbelief.

"How dare you speak to me like that, Anthony?" Francine shouted. "I gave you life, and I can take it away from you." As soon as the words were spoken, she clapped her hand over her mouth and cried, "I'm sorry, Anthony. I'm sorry." She began to sob.

"Forget it," he said.

Vinny put his arm around her, as she turned her face into his shoulder, muttering, "I'm sorry."

Anthony headed for the front door. "Vinny, come to my house later, and we'll strategize. At least there we can talk *privately*, without someone listening in." He slammed the door behind him.

Vinny arrived at his brother's house at seven o'clock. "Ma was really upset with you. You shouldn't talk to her that way, Ant. She means well."

"You're a wuss, Vin."

"Hey," his brother said, his anger rising. "You're the one who got us into this situation. Don't take it out on me. I was stupid to go along with you, and now, I'm the one who might go to prison for doing your dirty work."

If you had been washed out to sea, we wouldn't be in this mess, Anthony wanted to say.

"Who do you think ratted us out?" Vinny asked.

"Only you and me knew about our plan," Anthony said, his brow furrowed, his anger rising. "I didn't say nothing to anyone. Did you?" Vinny shook his head. "Unless ma told someone. She had that friggin baby monitor on listening to us."

"Ma wouldn't tell on us. She'd beat us senseless before saying anything," Vinny said. "After you left, she told me she thought we were playing a joke on her. Besides, what if she did tell someone, what are you going to do about it?"

Anthony stared at his brother. Identical twins. Identical thoughts.

"I ain't putting a pillow over her face while she's sleeping," Vinny yelled. "This is going too far, Ant."

"Okay, you're right; no use arguing over this," Anthony said. He walked to the refrigerator and got beers for them. "Sorry, man. I'm really stressed out."

Anthony showed his brother a list of places he called trying to find Jennifer. I talked to someone at "I Do" where she used to work. The woman never met Jennifer. She suggested I call Simone, and she gave me her number. I'll find out where she lives and drive by later. I'll bring flowers and say they're for Jennifer." Anthony snickered as he told Vinny the story of Simone's stalker who showed up with a big bouquet of red roses. "That'll scare the shit out of her. I'm looking forward to meeting the bitch face to face."

"You're evil," Vinny said jokingly. "Did you try Jennifer's apartment in Fairfield?"

"Yeah. I drove past it after I left ma's house. I knocked on the door, but no one answered. And before you got here, I called all the local hospitals. She ain't nowhere. I called Milford Hospital, St. Vincent's, Bridgeport Hospital, Yale New Haven, St. Raphael's, and Griffin Hospital. She ain't registered in any of them."

"Maybe they airlifted her to a hospital in Long Island," Vinny said.

"I didn't think of that. It don't matter anyway. By now, Jennifer probably blabbed to the cops about you leaving her there," Anthony said flippantly.

"She knew it was me, and not you," Vinny announced.

Anthony looked at his brother. "You didn't tell me that. You told her it was you, and not me?"

"No . . . no way, bro." She said, 'Anthony, where's your tattoo?'" Vinny paused for a moment then asked, "Do you have a tattoo, Anthony?"

"Nope," he answered quickly. "It must have been the combination of the pills and the wine. I ain't got no tattoo." Quickly switching subjects, Anthony said, "I also came up with a plan to get us off the hook. First, we have to get one of dad's shyster lawyers to represent us. Maybe someone who owes him a favor. Then, we have to create a story to tell the judge. And this time, we have to be precise with solutions to possible problems.

Thirty-Eight

Anthony arrived at work on Thursday morning, feeling anxious and sleep deprived from the recent events. The last two days, he had questioned his decision to leave Jennifer on Charles Island. Vinny should have tossed her into the water when he had a chance. He prayed the plan he and Vinny concocted would work.

He recalled his grandmother's voice, afflicted by broken English. "In Italy we have a saying: between two people, there's no such thing as a secret. One person has to be dead."

Anthony never considered what would happen if Jennifer survived, or that someone would have seen Vinny and her going out to the island. Who could have taken the photos, and why? Could he trust his brother? What would happen if he blabbed to the cops? *Between two people . . . no such thing as a secret.*

These were the questions that ran continuously in his mind.

At eleven-thirty, two police officers walked into Anthony's workplace. They met with the owner of the company behind closed doors. Fifteen minutes later, the boss called Anthony on his extension and asked him to come into his office. "I want to run something past you," he said.

"Sure, no problem," Anthony said, never suspecting what was about to happen.

When Anthony saw the two officers, he stopped short. "Is anything wrong? Is my mother okay?" he asked trying to buy time. "My father . . . brother . . ."

"Anthony Palmieri?" asked one of the officers.

"Yeah."

"You are under arrest for the attempted murder of Jennifer Keys." He read Anthony his rights, and slapped handcuffs on him.

"What's this all about?" Anthony said in a panic. "Where's Jennifer? What's happened to her? She left a note saying she was leaving me . . . that was two days ago . . . and I haven't heard from her since. Where is she? Is she okay?"

"Give up the act, Anthony," the other officer said as he escorted him past his fellow workers and out to the police car.

The remaining officer said he needed to interview the people in Anthony's section, to see if they had any knowledge of what happened.

"Sure . . . sure," his boss said anxiously. "Whatever you need to do. You can use my office. There's six people in his section, including him. Here are their names and extensions."

"Would it be okay with you, sir, if after we interview your employees, they are dismissed for the day? I'll have my partner escort them to their desk so they can get their personal belongings, and lead them out of the building. It is best they not go back and inform the others of what was discussed."

"No problem," he said.

One by one, the officers interviewed Anthony's co-workers. They were asked where they were on Tuesday, August twenty-seventh, and if they could say, without a doubt, that Anthony was at work that day. Each person told the story of how Anthony's twin, Vinny called his brother on his cell. One person said two o'clock, someone else said three-thirty, and the two others didn't remember the time. They all mentioned the two men spoke using FaceTime, and that Vinny agreed to meet a few of them at Stonebridge at six.

"Did either brother seem nervous?"

"No."

"Was the name Jennifer Keys mentioned?"

"No."

"Was Silver Sands State Park mentioned?"

"No."

"Was Charles Island mentioned?"

"No."

"Did Anthony or Vinny appear to be unusually nervous about anything?"

"No."

"Is there anything you'd like to tell us about that day?"

The questions continued: how long had they worked with Anthony? Did Vinny join them on a regular basis after work? Did anyone know of problems at home? The employees had more, or less, the same responses. Except for one person.

"Please state your name," the officer said.

"Felix Gerard."

The officer went through the same line of questioning, but when asked if he had anything to discuss about that day, Felix hesitated a few moments, and said, "Yes, I do."

He proceeded to say that, although Vinny said he was calling from where he worked, he was wearing a tank top, and there were trees in the background and a blue sky.

"He certainly didn't look like he was calling from work. Granted, he works at a gas station, but other times, he was wearing a Citco shirt."

Felix continued. "Then, when he showed up at Stonebridge, he was wearing a completely different outfit, and he looked as if he had just showered. It just seemed strange to me."

"Could it be that he left work, went home, showered, and changed clothes?" the officer asked.

"I guess so," Felix said, not considering that option. "In the past when he joined us after work, he'd be wearing his work clothes and smelling of gasoline. This time, something was different."

"Has Mr. Palmieri . . . Anthony, ever mentioned Jennifer Keys to you?"

"Yes. I've never met her, but he said she had been nagging him about getting married. He said he suspected she was seeing someone else on the side." Felix hesitated, then added. "Anthony said he followed her one day, and the guy she was with could have been a triplet."

"Did Mr. Palmieri say he thought his twin brother, Vinny might be having an affair with Jennifer?"

Felix stared at the cop. "No, he never said that he suspected his brother. But Anthony wasn't an angel, either."

"Continue, please."

Felix relayed the events of the evening at *The Cat's Meow,* and how friendly he was with the dancer. They got tattoos to remember the night, and Anthony got a tattoo with the woman's name. "In fact," he added, "I think that's what finally broke them up."

"Broke them up? Who? Anthony and the dancer?" the officer asked.

"No, Anthony and Jennifer. He said she left him a note on Tuesday morning that she was leaving him because of his partying, and not setting a wedding date. She took all her clothes, and her 'crap' – his word, not mine. She probably saw the name *Fran* tattooed in a heart on Anthony's ass."

"Mr. Gerard, you've been extremely helpful. Please leave us your contact information. We may need to ask you a few more questions. Rest assured, what was said here today will remain with us. And please do not discuss anything you told us with your co-workers. Thank you for your time."

After Felix left the office, the cop called his Captain and said, "We need to bring Vincent Palmieri in for questioning. And get warrants to confiscate the cell phones of Anthony and Vincent Palmieri."

When the police car parked in Francine Palmieri's driveway, Tara smiled while she watched through the lace curtains.

"How the mighty will fall," she said out loud, a satisfied look on her face.

The day before, Tara had gathered the dozen photographs she took of Vinny and Jennifer at Silver Sands Beach. Through her telephoto lens, she captured close ups of the couple meeting at the tombolo, walking out to Charles Island, and a photo of a man bobbing in the waters close to the island. Based on the diary entries, she was certain the man in the photos was Vinny, but he could easily pass for Anthony. The 8x10 photos, along with the brown diary (which she copied on her multi-use printer), were put into a large white envelope. She included a typed note:

> *I am not willing to be identified at this time. If it were to become necessary in the future, I am willing to give a statement.*

On the front of the envelope was typed:

GIVE TO MILFORD POLICE ASAP

While her husband Carmine slept, Tara slipped out of the house holding the envelope. In the darkness, she jogged to the local bakery, a brisk ten minutes away. She knew that at three o'clock a.m., the bakers would arrive to start creating their delicious delights for the day. She left the envelope on their front doorstep.

She did not pass anyone on the street. No cars drove by. The strip mall in front of the bakery was deserted. Her mission was completed with no one noticing her movements.

No one, except the camera on the house next door.

Thirty-Nine

She and her husband sat on the beach, enjoying the last rays of a colorful sunset spilling over the water.

"The summer is almost over," she said, with a tone of melancholy. "Labor Day is right around the corner. It's amazing how the older we get, the faster the days pass by."

He smiled and put his arm around her, protecting her from the on-shore breeze. Long shadows cast into Long Island Sound as the heads of the people walking disappeared into the waves. A young man walked along the shoreline. He carried a fishing pole in one hand, and a worn wicker basket filled with the day's catch over his shoulder. A small child, testing her independence, ran to the water, but she soon returned to the safety of her parents when her toes hit the end of the tepid water.

In the distance, they heard the sound of a motor boat as it slapped down hitting the water, followed by the bong of a buoy, and the caws of seagulls.

"This is my favorite time of the day," her husband said. "It's so peaceful."

Suddenly, the woman's cell phone played the first few bars of Beethoven's Fifth.

"It's Friday night, please don't answer it, her husband begged. "It's probably one of your crazy friends ready to jump off the Empire State Building because her daddy said 'no' to the Mercedes."

She chuckled. "I want to see whose calling." She looked at the caller id. It was a number she did not recognize. Curiosity took over.

"Let it go to voice mail," he begged.

"I'll make it quick, I promise. If it's a robo call, it'll be another number to block," she joked.

"Hello?" she said with some trepidation.

"Hello," the voice parroted on the other end. "This is Doctor Michael Brady from Yale New Haven Hospital. We have a patient here who refuses to tell us her name, unless she's allowed to talk to you."

The woman looked at her husband, tucked the phone under her chin, and whispered softly, "It's a doctor from Yale New Haven."

This piqued his interest. *Was a family member ill, in a car accident, or worse?*

His wife put the call on speaker, so they could both hear the conversation.

They continued to listen. "The patient was brought in late Tuesday night, unconscious, suffering from a concussion, severe abrasions and contusions. She is now stable, and able to talk to us. We are trying to contact her family, but she refuses to give us any information. Given she asked to call you, I feel confident she knows and trusts you. Would you be willing to talk to her?"

"Yes . . . yes, of course," answered the woman.

She took this opportunity to tell her husband, "I hope it's not one of your sisters who is in the hospital. Or, a prank."

The doctor held the phone up to Jennifer's ear. On the other end of the phone, the couple heard sobbing, then the doctor's voice, "You can do it. Take a deep breath. Here's a tissue . . . wipe your eyes . . . good . . . now, go on," he encouraged his patient.

"Hello?" the woman said to the mystery person on the other end. They waited for a response.

A whisper of a voice said, "Simone, I'm in trouble."

Forty

Simone and Charlie rushed to Jennifer's bedside. The two women cried when they saw each other. Jennifer was covered with bandages, bruises, and her right foot was in a cast. She had intravenous tubes hanging from two metal hangers. Machines noted blood pressure and oxygen levels.

"Well, you're a sight for sore eyes," Simone teased.

"So are you," Jennifer whispered. "Thank you for coming. Charlie, it's good to see you, too. It's good to see the two of you are still together."

Simone lifted her left hand and showed Jennifer her engagement ring, nestled with a simple gold wedding band. Charlie held up his hand to show her his wedding band.

"We got married only a few months ago. I wished you were there. You could have been my wedding planner," Simone joked.

Fresh tears burst forth, causing an alarm to go beep and notifying the nurse's station. Dr. Brady stepped into the room, and immediately checked on Jennifer. He flipped off a switch, checked her pulse, and handed her a tissue. "I seem to be the one drying your tears, young lady. Why are you crying this time? Do you miss me that much?" he joked.

He turned to Simone and Charlie. "You must be Simone," he said extending a hand. The three shook hands.

Simone noticed he had mesmerizing blue eyes that were the same color as Jennifer's. She refocused on his words. "She's one lucky woman. Longer exposure to the elements, and we might have had a different outcome."

He turned to Jennifer and asked, "May I steal your friends for a little while? I want to talk about you behind your back." He smiled at his patient.

She smiled back, and nodded. "I'd like to sleep now, if that's okay with you, Simone."

"Absolutely. Charlie and I will be back in a short while. You rest now." She gave her friend a gentle kiss on the forehead, and whispered, "It's good to see you, my friend. I've missed you."

Once inside the office, he told the couple, "We've contacted her mother. She and Jennifer's brother are on their way here."

"I'd like to be here when they arrive," Simone said. "I know Mrs. Keogh, and she'd find it a comfort knowing I'm helping her daughter. I don't know if Jennifer told you about her brother."

"Yes, she did," Doctor Brady said. He shook his head. "Sad."

"We didn't realize what had happened over the last few days. I was out of town working a wedding. It's only this evening, after your phone call, that I checked the news on our way here," Simone explained.

After a few moments, she said, "Doctor, my husband and I are concerned for Jennifer's safety. I fear Anthony and his family are vindictive. They have connections to people in high places, and I fear the twins will get off without any charges against them. And honestly, because of Jennifer's fragile state, I'm going to recommend that she lives where no one knows her whereabouts."

Doctor Brady agreed, and suggested that after her rehabilitation, she stay in a hotel, or with a friend until after the hearing.

"We could put her up in the Hamilton," Charlie said. "Or, she could live with you, Simone."

"Both places would be fine, Charlie, except Anthony knows about me, and those locations would be the first places where he would look. The same goes for her mother's home. We'll talk to Jennifer, and see if she has any thoughts."

"Do you have any idea when she'll be released from hospital?" Charlie asked.

"I'd give her at least another two or three days. I'd like to be able to get her off the machines, and eating some solid foods."

There was a knock on Dr. Brady's door. Nurse Stephanie popped her head in to announce that Mrs. Keogh and her son had arrived.

"Bring them in," he said.

Bridgette Keogh looked twenty years older since the last time Simone saw her, less than two years ago. She no longer had the "strong European look" Simone's mother used to like to say. "They work harder than American women, they have stronger blood and stronger hearts." Here stood a woman, no taller than 5'1", appearing frail and exhausted. Terrance, Jennifer's brother appeared to be sober, although years of drinking shown on his face, displaying a drinker's bulbous nose, covered with broken capillaries. *He's a high-functioning alcoholic,* Simone thought.

Hugs were exchanged. "Simone, I'm so happy to see you again," Mrs. Keogh said, the hint of her Irish brogue coming through. "You're the only steady rock in my daughter's life," the old woman said while gripping Simone's arm.

Simone assumed that Jennifer had never told her mother about their personal and business separation.

"Thank you, Mrs. Keogh. Now, you should talk to Dr. Brady. Charlie and I will be outside."

Dr. Brady explained Jennifer's injuries. He did not elaborate how she sustained them, who was with her, or where she was at the time. He simply said she had taken a fall while on a picnic, and she was now recovering. After all, unless Jennifer agreed to let her mother know her medical history, as she had agreed for Simone, the doctor was limited to how much information he could release.

He then took Mrs. Keogh and Terrance to see the patient. She cried when she saw Jennifer. "My daughter . . . my daughter . . . I'm so sorry."

"No, mama. I'm sorry," Jennifer said. "You were right. I played with the devil and he almost ate me. You were right about Anthony. He is not a good man."

"Did he hit you?" she asked, immediately concerned. She looked at the doctor, questioning the story he told her.

Doctor Brady jumped in and said, "As I told you Mrs. Keogh, Jennifer was at a picnic, and she fell and sustained injuries." He looked at Jennifer, his eyes saying: *don't worry, I'll protect you.*

"Yes, mama, I fell at a picnic," Jennifer reported.

Meanwhile, in the hallway, Simone and Charlie discussed where Jennifer was going to live while she recuperated, and a permanent home was established. Charlie again mentioned the Hamilton Hotel, but just as quickly agreed with Simone that she would not be safe there, especially if his nephew, Frederick found out. They would discuss it with Jennifer after her mother left.

Shortly after Mrs. Keogh and Terrance left the hospital and headed back to their home in Long Island, Dr. Brady informed Simone that Jennifer wanted to talk to her. The couple walked into her room. Jennifer was sitting up, looking notably better. Her eyes lit up when she saw her friend.

"So Charlie, you finally made an honest woman out of Simone," Jennifer joked. Then quickly added, "Sorry, it's the drugs talking."

"No need to apologize," he said. Charlie told her his divorce had become finalized in December. He followed with the romantic proposal, and the even-more romantic story about the first wedding in front of the Eiffel Tower, followed by the small reception at the Grand Hamilton Hotel.

"I wish I had been there," Jennifer said, her blue eyes twinkling.

"Us, too," Simone said, looking up at Charlie. He put his arm around his wife and smiled.

"Enough of this mushy stuff," Simone said. "We need to find a safe place for you to live, and where Anthony can't find you. Charlie thought about the Hamilton Hotel, but you know what a big mouth Frederick is, so that won't work. We thought about my house, but it has a lot of steps, and Anthony can easily find the address."

"What about where I am now? He can call the hospitals and find me."

"No, he won't. You're registered under Jane Doe because you didn't have any identification with you, and Dr. Blue-Eyes promised he'd keep your name safe. Besides, there's a police officer outside your door 24/7."

Simone added, "Also, I would not recommend you going back to your house for a while."

Jennifer noticed a sly grin on Simone's face . . . a look she knew well from the years they worked together. "Simone, what have you done to my house?" Jennifer asked, fearing the answer.

Simone looked at Charlie, then back at Jennifer and smiled. "I'm going to buy it. Lock, stock and barrel! I will have him evicted."

"You'll do what?" Jennifer shouted, causing fresh pain to flow through her head. "How will you do that . . . why will you do that . . . ?"

Simone filled Jennifer in on the details. "Apparently, the mortgage hadn't been paid for several months, nor the real estate taxes. The house is going into foreclosure next month."

Jennifer's mouth dropped open. She mumbled, "I had no idea. None, whatsoever. Anthony was in charge of paying those bills. We shared expenses 50/50 and I always gave him my share of money towards the mortgage and taxes. That son-of-a-bitch."

The pieces of the puzzle began fitting together, and she concluded, "Simone, I think Anthony and Vinny were in on this together. They wanted to kill me because then Anthony would inherit the house, my life insurance, and any money in the bank. He'd gladly walk away from that house and live in the Cayman Islands, thinking he was free and rich."

"Yes, we thought that as well. But now, I'll own the house under an LLC. He'll never know who the owner is."

"What if he has a lawyer research the owner's name? Although it's under an LLC, the Managing Member has to be listed."

"He'll never figure out that Alison S. Deschamps is I. I'm putting the purchase under my maiden name. Trust me, it won't be easy, but Sid Harding is a miracle worker. After the house is purchased and completely renovated by Pete, the contractor, you can move in and live there for as long as you wish."

Jennifer continued to shake her head in amazement at her friend, although the movement caused new pain. Tears began flowing again. "Simone, you don't have to do this for me. I wasn't very nice to you."

"Shush, don't you fret," Simone said. "The only thing you need to worry about now is getting well, and finding yourself a place to live. Got any ideas?"

Jennifer reflected, then said, "I met a new friend at the beach. Her name is Mary Ann. She lives in an apartment on Melba Street, not far from me. She and her husband travel a lot. They go to Florida for the winter, so maybe I can stay there for a while, and house sit while they're away."

She gave Simone Mary Ann's last name, and address. "Simone, I have no idea where my cell phone is. In fact, I don't know where my car is, as I left it in the parking lot at Silver Sands. It's probably been towed. There's not much I remember of that day."

"As I said, all you have to worry about right now is getting better. I'll call Mary Ann and see if she can help us. I'm sure by now, she's heard the news of Anthony and Vinny's arrest for the attempted murder of Jennifer Keys."

"Oh no, Simone. Really? I was on the news? And I didn't have any mascara or high heels on!"

"Oh honey, those drugs are really making you wacky," Simone joked.

She and Charlie kissed Jennifer goodbye, and promised to come back the next day. "I'll update you once I talk to Mary Ann. And tell Doctor Dreamy-Eyes I'll see him when you are discharged."

Jennifer blushed. "He *is* cute, isn't he?" she said.

Forty-One

The next day, Simone called Mary Ann, introduced herself, and explained the details about Jennifer's situation. She was comforted to know Jennifer was safe, and away from "that monster." She told Simone she had never met Anthony, but didn't like him solely on what Jennifer had told her about him. Mary Ann had heard the news on the TV, but it seemed Jennifer wasn't registered at any of the hospitals she had called. She expressed her concern for her friend, and was pleased to know she'll be fine.

Simone updated Mary Ann, telling her Jennifer's need for a place to live where Anthony couldn't find her. Ideally, somewhere with few, or no steps.

Mary Ann said, "I told Jennifer that I had a lot of problems with my feet and legs because of high heels. I'm not surprised she's sustained a broken ankle." She paused for a few seconds. "I'll need to talk to my husband. I doubt he would object to having Jennifer live here while she recovers. She can have our master bedroom with an en suite. Since we travel a lot, she'll have the place to herself most days. I'm happy to help, Simone. Again, let me ask Greg before I agree."

"Absolutely," Simone said. "I understand completely. And, Mary Ann, don't make your husband feel pressured. He needs to be fully on board. We do have Option B, if necessary. My husband works at a hotel, so he might be able to have her stay there under an alias."

"I'll get back to you by tomorrow morning," Mary Ann promised.

"Thanks. Oh, and Jennifer sends her regards. She promises to take care of herself so that next summer the two of you can walk the beach again."

Mary Ann called Simone back within the hour. "Simone, my husband said 'yes' without any provocation by me. He suggested you come over this evening, if possible, so we can all meet and discuss what's expected of us."

"Thank you. Is eight-thirty good? I hope that's not too late."

"Not at all. We're night owls. See you this evening. By the way, do you drink coffee – I have decaf, if you want."

"Coffee?" Simone chuckled. "Like Jennifer's obsession with spike heels, coffee is mine."

Charlie and Simone arrived at Mary Ann's apartment promptly at eight-thirty. They climbed the three steps into the main lobby, and took the elevator to the second floor. "Jennifer can easily do those steps," Charlie said. "Especially if she has an aide with her."

The foursome introduced themselves to each other. "Thank you so much for offering to help Jennifer," Charlie said.

Delicious, freshly brewed coffee and mini crumb cakes were offered. Simone wasn't shy about indulging.

Mary Ann gave Simone and Charlie a tour of their apartment. "We think Jennifer will be safe here. No one can enter the building without the code, or being buzzed in."

The apartment was decorated with nautical accents, sea glass greens and blues were the dominate colors of the furniture that sat on light-colored birch flooring. Large sculptures of seabirds, seahorses and mermaids filled the space. "Your apartment is wonderful," Charlie said. "It's so inviting, and I love the location."

"We think the bedroom is large enough for Jennifer to work with the physical therapist," Mary Ann said.

Greg added, "I think Jennifer will love the screened-in patio. Each room has a view of the water, but the patio is a wonderful spot to read, relax and heal."

The couples discussed timing. It was agreed that Jennifer would arrive directly from the hospital. Simone would purchased new outfits for her friend, as she wouldn't dare try to take anything from the house. She'd also provide her with a new cell phone, and any necessities.

"We'd like to pay a stipend for housing Jennifer," Simone added. After refusing any monies, Simone reminded them there is a cost for their friend to live there – food, laundry, electricity. "I insist," Simone said.

Before leaving Simone said, "I have one more question: are you allowed to have pets here? If so, would you allow Jennifer to have a therapy dog?"

The couple were taken aback by this question. They both loved dogs, and would have had one except they traveled so frequently.

"Think about it," Simone said. "Of course, if there is any damage whatsoever, I'll reimburse you. Please, don't answer now. I also have to speak to her doctor to see if he thinks she'll need one. After what she's been through, a support animal might accelerate the healing process."

Back in the car, Charlie asked, "What was that about a dog?"

"I have an idea, Charlie, but I'm not sure it'll work."

Forty-Two

Jennifer was discharged from the hospital nine days after her harrowing experience, and moved directly into Mary Ann's 1275 square foot apartment. She managed quite well on crutches getting up the three steps leading into the lobby. Charlie stood close by just in case she staggered. She immediately fell in love with the location, and the views of the water. "Oh, Mary Ann and Greg, thank you so much. This is so beautiful. I love your beach décor."

It didn't take Jennifer long to settle into her new surroundings. A physical therapist came the next day, and worked with Jennifer doing exercises focused mainly on her legs, as she was still experiencing severe leg cramps. "Once your ankle heals," the therapist said, "we'll work on helping to regain your balance."

Jennifer was a perfect patient. She did her exercises as instructed, took her medications, and rested in bed. The closet was filled with new clothes, and 'smart' but comfortable new shoes. "Geez, Simone, I'm going to look like an old lady in those things," she whined.

"Get over it, girlfriend. No more stilettos for you."

"Are you okay, Simone?" Jennifer asked her friend as Simone reached out to grab the bedpost.

"Yes, I just had a dizzy spell, that's all. The heat, excitement, and I guess I bent over too quickly to admire your new shoes," she laughed.

"You know, Simone," Jennifer said with a serious tone, "you don't have to do all this for me. Once I'm better and back at my job, I'll buy some outfits. And I insist on reimbursing you for the clothes, the iPhone, the house . . . everything."

"It is going to be a long time before you can return to work," Simone reminded her friend. "Besides, you need new outfits now for your follow-up examinations with Dr. Brady."

"He *is* cute," Jennifer said. "I wonder if he's married."

"Why not ask him?" Simone suggested.

"I don't know. After this past nightmare with Anthony, I'm not ready to date anyone. Besides, I don't think he'd be allowed to date a patient," Jennifer said. "He does have a great bedside manner, don't you think?"

"Yes, he does," Simone agreed. "I'm sure you noticed he wasn't wearing a wedding band," she added.

"I'm usually the one to pay attention to wedding bands, Simone. I didn't this time."

"You're losing your touch, my friend. Seriously, I think he likes you, Jennifer. The two times I've taken you to your follow-up appointments, he seemed very friendly. But you're correct, he's not allowed to date a patient. But when you're healed, and no longer his patient, maybe you can ask him to meet for coffee."

"I'll think about it, Simone. Right now, I just want to focus on getting well, and dealing with the horror of wearing those ugly shoes you bought for me," Jennifer joked.

Forty-Three

Anthony returned to work the following Monday morning after bail was posted. Felix, and the others in the office, kept their distance from him. No one mentioned the incident under strict orders from the company owner. Tensions ran high.

On Friday morning, an official-looking man appeared in front of Anthony's desk. His co-workers stopped what they were doing, anticipating another arrest, as they watched and listened.

"Anthony Michael Palmieri?" asked the man.

"Yeah," Anthony said, expecting the man to pull handcuffs out of his pocket.

"Consider yourself served." The man turned and walked away.

Inside the envelope was a notice that his house was now owned by the bank. He had twenty-four hours to remove his personal possessions. After that, he would be considered trespassing, arrested and charged.

"Shit," he mumbled.

No one, including Felix, asked about the letter. Nor, did they want to get involved. Everyone went back to doing their job.

Anthony showed up at Francine's house, suitcases and dog in tow. "Ma, I got thrown out of my own house. Can you believe it? I bet Jennifer had something to do with this."

Anthony showed his mother the letter. Francine said, "It states you didn't pay the mortgage or taxes. What did you expect? Of course, they're going to throw you out. If you didn't have the money, you could have come to us."

"I didn't have the money because I was paying you and dad back for the down payment," Anthony snapped.

Suddenly, she became quiet. She couldn't deny it any longer. Everything she had heard on the monitor was true. Anthony had planned to inherit the house from Jennifer, and her bank account money, which he'd use to pay the overdue mortgage and taxes. She loved her son, but right now, she was fed up.

She looked at Anthony with disgust, and Goober with resignation. "I don't want that smelly mutt in my house."

Goober whined.

"But I don't have any place to go."

"You can live in the basement with your brother. You two are thick as thieves, and now you can learn how to live together."

Begrudgingly, Anthony moved his possessions and his dog into Vinny's domain. Neither twin was happy being in close quarters with a smelly, depressed dog.

"What's wrong with him?" asked Vinny.

"I don't know. He doesn't want to eat. He just sits around all day looking pathetic."

"Maybe he's sick. Or, maybe he misses Jennifer."

At the mention of her name, Goober stood up, his ears darted skyward, and he began barking.

"Shut up, you damn mutt," Anthony shouted. "Go lay down."

The dog cowered.

"I'm sick of him," Anthony said. "Without . . . you know who around . . . he's nothing more than a pain in the ass. He doesn't even want to run around at the beach."

"He misses her," Vinny said. "Actually, Ant, I'm sorry I listened to you and took her out there. It was a big mistake."

This declaration didn't surprise Anthony. Although Vinny was his identical twin, he wasn't like him at all – daring, scheming, and adventurous. No, Vinny was a wuss. *That's what you get for living with mommy all these years,* he decided.

Forty-Four

A hearing was scheduled for three weeks after the incident. Meanwhile, Anthony and Vinny remained free on one million dollars bail. His father used their home, and their retirement money as collateral.

The defendant, Jennifer Keys was not in attendance because she was recovering in an undisclosed rehabilitation facility. Her attorney, Sidney Harding represented his client.

In the courtroom were Anthony and Vinny's parents, their sisters and husbands. In the upstairs gallery and in the back row sat Simone Simpson.

After Vinny was sworn in, his attorney asked, "Please state your full name."

"Vincent Michael Palmieri."

Follow up questions about his age, address, and place of employment were asked. "Can you tell us where you were on August twenty-seventh at approximately four o'clock in the afternoon?"

Vinny hesitated, looked at Anthony, and said, "I was on Charles Island."

Collective whispers were heard in the courtroom. The judge banged his gavel.

"Were you alone on Charles Island?"

Again, Vinny looked at Anthony, bowed his head and whispered, "No, I wasn't."

"Can you tell the court who you were with."

"I was with Jennifer Keys."

Repeated banging of the gavel echoed throughout in the room. Sobs resounded by Francine and the twins' siblings.

"And can you tell me what you were doing there with Ms. Keys."

Vinny didn't answer.

"I'll repeat the question. What were you and Ms. Keys doing on Charles Island together?"

Vinny again looked at Anthony, and mouthed, *Sorry.* He whispered, "We were having sex."

"Can you repeat your answer so the court can hear you?"

In a louder voice he answered, "We were having sex."

More banging of the gavel to quiet the audience.

"Is this the first time you and Jennifer went to Charles Island?"

"Yes."

"And, is this the first time you and Jennifer had sex on Charles Island?"

"Yes."

Sid Harding was acutely aware that Vinny's attorney did not ask if this was the first time they had sex. Rather, was it the first time they had sex on Charles Island.

Vinny stared soberly at Anthony, but his brother kept his head bowed.

"Was this a planned adventure?"

"Yeah . . . I mean, yes. When Anthony and I were younger, we used to swap places with our girlfriends, teachers and even our parents. It was fun then, but I never thought it would come to this." Again, he looked at Anthony and said, "I'm sorry, bro."

"Can you tell us what actually happened that day?"

Meanwhile, Sid Harding didn't object, because there was no point. He had information he'd reveal at the appropriate time. He enjoyed watching Vinny squirm on the stand.

Vinny answered, "Her and me went to Charles Island to have a picnic. We had some wine and cheese." He paused for effect. "Then, we had sex."

"Continue," his attorney ordered.

Anthony's head was still lowered. He began moving it from side to side, pretending he couldn't believe what he was hearing. As if on cue, the two twins removed handkerchiefs from their back pockets, and blew their nose.

Identical twins.

Rehearsed act.

"Please tell us what happened next," his attorney continued.

"I told her I couldn't do this behind my brother's back. I told her I didn't want to see her no more, and that I wanted to break up with her. We got into a heated argument. She tried slapping me, but I grabbed her arm - yeah, I did - and she fell down. I tried to help her up, but she screamed and said to leave her alone. She got crazy. Real crazy. She started hitting and kicking me. She screamed, "You're just like your brother.""

Vinny chuckled at this last line, looked at the judge and said, "We're identical twins." He turned back to his attorney and added, "Like, duh."

"Mr. Palmieri," said the judge, "please avoid commentary."

"Sorry, judge." Vinny paused, looking like a hurt little boy.

"Continue," his attorney said.

"So, as I was saying, when I looked at the time, I realized we needed to get off the island because the tide was coming in. She didn't want to come with me. I begged her. I told her she needed to leave, but she just kept on yelling at me. It was horrible. I hate to admit it, but I left her there. I wasn't going to hang around with a crazy woman. So I found my way back to the opening in the chicken wire, jumped into the water, and swam back to land."

At the appropriate moment, Simone left the courtroom, found a bailiff, and handed him a note to give to Sid Harding. It was marked, 'urgent.' Simone informed him, "I need for you to wait until Mr. Harding is almost finished. When he asks Mr. Palmieri about his clothes."

"Excuse me?" asked the court officer.

"Please," begged Simone. "It is important you wait until then."

The Palmieri twins weren't the only ones who could perform a rehearsed move.

The twins locked eyes. Vinny said, "Bro, I'm sorry I hurt you. I really am."

The judge instructed Vinny's attorney to control his client from speaking to his brother.

Calculated questions were posed by the Palmieri attorney, making it look as if Jennifer made an independent decision to stay on the island.

Next, it was Sidney Harding's turn to interview the defendant.

"Mr. Palmieri, can you explain why you called your brother using FaceTime from Charles Island?"

"I called Anthony right after Jennifer started acting crazy. I wanted to tell him about Jennifer, and me . . . I wanted everything to come out in the open . . . to clear my conscious. So I called him, and he asked me to join him at Stonebridge."

"How is it you were able to swim back to the beach, and show up in clean clothes? Were the clothes in your car as part of the plan to leave Jennifer on the island?"

"Objection," shouted Vinny's attorney.

"I withdraw the question," Sid said.

The bailiff stood in the back of the room. Once Mr. Harding asked Vinny about his clothes in the car, he walked up to the attorney and handed him the note.

"I don't mind answering the question," said Vinny, while Sid was momentarily interrupted.

"I always have a change of clothes in my car," said Vinny. "In case I go out directly after work. So, I changed my clothes and met Anthony at the restaurant." Going against the judge's order, Vinny looked at his brother and said, "I'm so sorry, Anthony."

"If you speak to your brother one more time, I'll find you in contempt of court," the judge warned Vinny.

After Sid Harding read the note, he asked, "Judge, may I approach the bench?" Meanwhile, Simone slipped back into her seat.

The two attorneys conferred with the judge. Harding showed the judge the hand-written, notarized note:

> I, Jennifer Keys am not able to attend today's hearing as I am recovering in an undisclosed location. To preserve my mental and physical health, I do not wish to press charges against Anthony or Vincent Palmieri. I want my life back. I do not wish to see or communicate with the two men ever again. I ask the court to grant me permanent protection orders against Anthony and Vincent Palmieri.

"Given this new evidence, I have no other choice." The judge banged his gavel and said, "Case dismissed."

He turned to Sid and said, "Mr. Harding, please see me in my chambers to discuss the request in this letter."

The brothers ran to each other, and fell into each other's arms. Joyful tears and apologies permeated the courtroom. Francine pushed her way through the crowd, hugged her two boys and cried, "My babies. My babies."

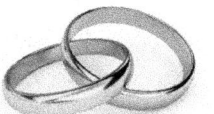

Forty-Five

A few days later, Anthony returned to work, relieved to be free of the past nightmare. He still faced a long road ahead: how to repay his attorney, his parents, and where was he going to find a place to live on his salary. Add to that his bad credit, he'd be living with his parents for years.

As he sat at his desk, punching in numbers on his computer, a man walked up to him, dropped a sealed envelope in front of him, and left. *That was easy,* thought Charlie, as he got in his car and drove away.

"Who was that?" Anthony asked Felix. But his former drinking buddy just shrugged his shoulders.

Anthony opened the letter, and couldn't believe his luck:

I will pay you $5,000 cash for your dog, Goober. Meet me this evening at seven sharp in front of Home Depot on Orange Avenue. No questions asked. Any attempt to notify the police will cause you additional time in the courts. I will obtain access to the camera recordings in front of the store, proving you sold your dog.

With Goober on a leash, Anthony stood in front of Home Depot waiting. At seven o'clock sharp as promised, a woman approached Anthony. She wore oversized sunglasses, a large floppy hat, and bright red lipstick. She handed him the envelope, and Anthony handed her the leash.

He opened the envelope, and glanced at the bills.

"It's all there. Now get in your car and drive away," she ordered.

Anthony drove off without any regret or ill feelings. He was just happy to be relieved of the animal.

"Ma, he said when he got home, I have some bad news for you."

"Now what did you do?" Francine asked, her hands on her hips.

"I accidently left the front door open when I was going to walk Goober. I forgot my cell phone, went downstairs for it, and when I came back, he was gone. I looked everywhere, but I can't find him."

Francine didn't know if she should laugh, cheer or appear to act sad. She said nothing. She turned around, went back to washing dishes, and allowed a large smile to dominate her face.

Yes, in the Palmieri Family, secrets were sacred.

Back in the Porsche, Goober jumped into the back seat. He whined a bit, and slobbered all over Simone's car. She removed the hat and sunglasses, and headed directly to the doggie camp. Here Goober would stay for four days, becoming trained in being an ESA. He had obedience struggles, but the trainers were patient, and he was a great student.

At the end of his training, two women arrived at the facility. One walked with a cane while she held onto the arm of her companion. When Goober recognized them, he gave out a long, soulful howl that caused the trainers to stop what they were doing. Some of the other dogs cowered, and backed up against the wall. Others howled in unison with Goober. Their wolf ancestry came forth with unity for their brother.

"It's okay boy," the trainer said, releasing him from his sitting position.

Goober charged towards Jennifer, who was now kneeling with open arms. He jumped, barked and licked her face as if she were a giant ice cream cone. If it were possible for a dog to cry, Goober would have been bawling with delight, just like Jennifer and Simone.

"Hello, Goober," Simone said, her voice cracking with emotion. She too was treated to slobbery licks.

The reunion was emotional for everyone at the facility. The team of trainers explained the commands to the two women. "He might require a few more classes to tweak what he learned. He was a delight, once we got him to obey the commands. He is certainly happy to see you," the trainer said as she patted the dog's head.

"Come on, Goober, let's go home," Jennifer said.

He walked slowly next to Jennifer, obeying her command not to pull. "Sit," she said until Simone opened the door. He jumped in at her instructions. Then Simone helped her friend into the front seat. They drove toward the apartment by the beach.

"Soon," Simone said, "you and Goober will be back in your old house. The transaction is going much faster than Sid thought it would. And, Pete thinks he'll have the house ready for you in four weeks."

"How can I repay you, Simone? You've done so much for me."

"It's my pleasure. I wanted to do this for you. Consider it a bribe to get you back to working at "I Do" after you're healed."

"Seriously? You want me back?"

"Of course. I'd love to work with you again. A lot has changed since your left. And when you're up to it, I'll fill you in on the details. But right now, you need to get your pup home. It's been an emotional day for all of us."

Jennifer was surprised to see how well-trained Goober had become. He didn't jump up on people, or on the bed – unless invited.

As the days passed, the nurse's aide, Jennifer and Goober were seen walking the parking lot of the apartment building. They'd walk down the concrete steps to the water, and stroll along the sand. Goober refrained from running after gulls, geese, or digging for sand crabs. He was now a 'working dog.'

Her healing was progressing nicely. After a few weeks, she no longer needed the cane, and the aide came only two days a week, to drive Jennifer to follow-up doctor appointments, grocery shopping, or for a ride away from Milford.

Jennifer was granted a protection order against Anthony and Vinny, and she was instructed that at any time she was approached by anyone mentioning the twins' names, she was to call 911.

Simone visited Jennifer every day. "You look a little gray," Jennifer said.

"I had a dizzy spell again the other day, and just now riding up in the elevator."

"Simone, you know you don't need to come here every day. It's not exactly around the corner from where you live. It's twenty-five minutes from your home to here," scolded Jennifer. "Are you drinking enough water? Maybe you're dehydrated."

"I'm drinking enough coffee," Simone joked. "You're right. I'm not drinking enough water, and the Indian summer days make it difficult to know what to wear.

"How about you call me every day, instead of driving up here? I have Goober now, and he's a great protector."

They agreed Simone would call every day, and visit when needed.

Forty-Six

"Hey Carmine, are you related to the Palmier twins?" his boss asked him.

"Yeah, they're my brother's kids."

"I thought so. You all sort of look alike.'

Go to hell, is what Carmine wanted to say. Instead, he inquired, "Why do you ask?"

"I saw them at the batting cages the other day – the ones in Monroe – and they had on shirts that said, *Palmieri Twins.* They're very good, just like you. I want you to invite them to join our team. We can use guys like that. Maybe it'll get us to the World Series of Softball."

Carmine was stunned by this request. No, it was a direct order, but all he could say was, "That's a great idea, Jack. I'll talk to them tonight." *Crap,* he thought.

While Tara prepared dinner, Carmine told her that his boss wanted the brats to join their softball league. "I told him I'd ask them tonight. If I don't talk to them, and Jack runs into them at the batting cages again, he'll want to know why they declined the offer. The last thing I want to do is go over there and ring their doorbell."

Tara suggested Carmine leave a note on Vinny's car window. Tell them the truth that it was Jack who invited them, and not you.

"You know, for a dumb blond, you're not so stupid after all," Carmine said.

This remark hit Tara like a slap across the face. She slammed down his dinner plate in front of him, and left the room.

"Hey, ain't you going to eat?" he asked.

"I'm no longer hungry," she shouted back. *I hope you choke on the pork chop,* is what she wanted to say.

Carmine left a note on Vinny's car, tucked under the wiper. He included Jack's full name and number, and instructed him to call his boss directly, noting that he had nothing to do with this offer.

Vinny told Anthony about the note from Carmine. "How about we try out for a team that plays against Carmine's?" said Anthony. "Who the hell would want to play with him – we'd want to play against him."

"Who do we call about opposing teams?" asked Vinny.

"I don't know. I'll do some research at work tomorrow."

"I know who to call," said the voice listening on the baby monitor.

Forty-Seven

Anthony's cell phone rang at work. He didn't recognize the number, so he let it go to voice mail. It rang again, and then a third time. Finally, he picked up. "Hello."

"This is Gertie," the woman said with a deep southern drawl. "I'm the secretary to the scout for the Pawtucket Red Sox Minor League Team. Is this Anthony Palmieri?"

"Yeah."

"My boss saw you and your brother at the New Haven game the other night. He asked me to inform you he wants you boys to try out for our team. He said to meet him by the back door after tonight's game. Don't tell anyone you're meeting him 'cause he ain't hiring no other players. He said the other players suck. His word, not mine."

"Really? He saw us play? That's great," Anthony said with excitement.

"Yes, he did. Tonight after the game."

"What's your boss' name?"

But the woman had disconnected the call.

After that evening's game, the twins took their time getting dressed. Everyone needed to leave before them, so neither one would have to explain why they were hanging around. They took leisurely showers, shaved, and were the last ones to leave the locker room. They waved good night to the janitor, who was swaying to the music emanating from his earbuds.

He waved back, gave them an expansive grin, showing off large, bright white teeth too large for his mouth. "Night boys," he shouted over his music.

Vinny and Anthony stood outside the back entrance waiting for the scout to show. "Do you know what he looks like?" Vinny asked. "Or, what his name is?"

"Not a clue. He just said he saw us play and wants us to try out. I wonder if he knows Uncle Carmine's boss; maybe he recommended us. He'll be here, I'm sure." Anthony was beginning to feel a little foolish. What if it was a joke a team member was playing on them?

From behind a dumpster walked a figure dressed in black. It was a woman (they assumed) in a burqa, with only her dark black eyes exposed. She walked towards them, and stopped a few feet in front of them.

"What's your problem, rag head?" Anthony asked. "Can't you see we're busy?"

His brother Vinny poked him, and whispered, "Hey, that's not nice. Maybe she's lost or something."

Anthony just shrugged.

She didn't answer but just continued to stare.

"What?" Anthony screamed at her. "What do you want? Get lost."

The woman focused on Anthony's words. Suddenly, from under her long garment she drew out a Louisville slugger baseball bat. The ash wood contrasted against her black gloves. Without warning, she swung the bat, hitting Anthony's knees first then Vinny's. Both men went down in agonizing pain.

"Stop!" they screamed. They were unable to stand. Anthony's arms reached up, and tried to grab her long dress, but she stepped back in time. He looked like an injured giant crab scurrying along on his broken knees.

She never spoke. She hit Vinny's left arm, and he cried for her to stop. Then she smacked Anthony's arm, hard enough for the sound of breaking bones to echo through the alley.

Next, their shoulders, breaking clavicles, and rotator cuffs.

She paused, and took in deep breaths. Finally, she spoke. "I am not going to hit your brain because I want you to know the pain you are experiencing."

She went back to her mission. She swung the bat across their backs with crushing sounds of ribs breaking.

"Please, stop," begged Anthony. "Why are you doing this? Who are you?" He began to spit up blood.

But the woman never answered. Instead, she said, "I want you to know the fright and danger of being left for dead."

She looked down at Vinny and Anthony writhing in pain. Her smile reached her eyes – the only thing the boys saw.

Making sure no one was approaching, she listened to their wallowing cries of pain. She enjoyed watching as the scene unfolded. The brothers lay in crumpled heaps. Barely conscious, Anthony looked up at the mystery woman and pleaded for his life to be spared.

"Stop. Please. I'm begging you." The same sentiment was parroted by Vinny.

"You were born together, and you'll die together."

As the final blows came, each hit was connected to a name. "This one is for Carmine, and this one is for Veronica, and this one is for Tara."

Teeth were crushed, eye sockets busted, and noses shattered.

Vinny was near death.

A final moan came from Anthony.

"And this one, Anthony, is for what you did to Jennifer," she said slamming the final blow.

She turned away from the gruesome scene, got in her car and drove away.

Afterwards, the woman drove to the Shelton Walmart, twenty-five miles from her home. She navigated her car behind the main entrance, and followed signs for the loading docks. She glanced up, looked for security cameras, and found one hanging from frayed wires. *Good, they didn't fix it.* It most likely had been smashed by an eighteen wheeler backing in, preparing to unload its cargo.

She slowed the car, being mindful of dock workers, although at that hour of the night, the chances of anyone being there was slim. The woman shut off the headlights, coasted up to the dumpsters, and double checked that the interior light was pushed to the off position. Quickly walking to the dumpsters, she opened the lid of the recycle bin and deposited the baseball bat. In the other bin was tossed the burqa. Just as swiftly, she got in her car, buckled up, and headed towards the mall's exit. Frequently, she looked in the rear view mirror to be sure no one was following her. It wasn't until she got onto the Merritt Parkway that she realized her shoulders were so tense they almost reached her earlobes. She inhaled a relaxing breath, exhaled, and repeated the process several more times. Despite the stress of the evening, the results were worth it. *Those twins deserved the beatings.*

Her anxiety level heightened again when she thought about her husband, Carmine. He had a game tonight, ironically enough, against the Palmieri twins, but then she realized he might be questioned by the police. After all, he did have a grudge against their family, and he was at the game tonight, with access to the locker room. He might not even be home yet.

If he was at home, what excuse would she use for coming in so late? She'd say she had to babysit their grandchild, or one of her friends needed a sympathetic ear. Several excuses raced through her mind. She chided herself for not thinking about this earlier, but it was too late now. She hoped Carmine would be sound asleep in front of the TV, as he was most nights.

As quietly as possible she opened the front door, holding the jumble of house keys tightly in her hand so they wouldn't clink. She stood in the entranceway and listened. Carmine's snoring blanketed the voice of a TV newscaster. Tara removed her shoes, and like a prowling cat, she crept upstairs, making sure to skip the third stair that squeaked.

Upstairs, she undressed and tossed her clothes haphazardly inside her closet. She tiptoed into the bathroom, took out the dark contact lenses and dropped them into the toilet. They floated like two eyeballs of an escaped Floridian snake, finding its way into someone's toilet bowl. She used a facecloth to scrub the dark makeup from her face, and tossed the stained cloth into the laundry basket. She stood still and listened. An announcer was informing the listening audience of the possible side effects from the latest and greatest drug being promoted. "Warning: this drug could cause seizures, confusion, hallucinations, and even death." *Geez*, though Tara, *why not tell the patient to just walk in front of a train.*

The commercial ended and a symphony of augmented triads began: the theme song of the show and Carmine's snoring. She turned on the lamp on his side of the bed, shut her light, climbed under the sheets, and was asleep within minutes.

Sometime later, she heard Carmine came to bed. She pretended to be asleep, in no mood for a third degree about her whereabouts, or why she didn't wake him. She heard him drop his clothes at the foot of the bed, emit a loud yawn, and soon the snoring concert began again. *I'm sorry I left the baseball bat behind. I could use it right about now,* she thought.

This evening was one of her greatest accomplishments. It's too bad she could never share her victories with another soul as long as she lived.

No, the Palmieri family had many secrets to keep.

Forty-Eight

Jennifer's recovery was quicker than she or her doctors thought possible. She was convinced that Goober played a large role. Although he was once a burden, she now found him to be a loving and trusting companion. Wherever she went, he tagged along. Since he was a therapy dog, he was allowed to accompany her in stores, and a few restaurants with outdoor seating. She knew there would come a time when she would have to leave him home alone, but she'd worry about that later. Right now, she just wanted to enjoy her newly renovated surroundings, and be reunited with her dog.

Soon it was moving day from Mary Ann's apartment to the beach house in Woodmont, transformed into a fairy tale home. Pete Cody, and Simone's interior designer, did a superb job of making her home pet-friendly, and accessible to Jennifer's immediate needs. Pete took an old sunroom and transformed it into a master suite. On days when Jennifer's legs were tired, or cramping, she could stay downstairs, instead of having to climb the stairs to the bedrooms. In the future, it would be a lovely guest room.

During the renovations, Pete found three suitcases and garbage bags filled with Jennifer's belongings. He informed Simone of his findings. She recommended he incorporate the clothes – not the shoes – in her closet with her new outfits, and place her knickknacks throughout the home.

Part of Jennifer's healing process was forgiving the people who hurt her. She could never forgive Anthony or Vinny for their plan to kill her. And now that they were holding on to life with a thread, the other family members must think she hates them as well. She wrote a note addressed to Francine, which she wanted Simone to read before sending.

"You must be so excited to be back in your home," Simone told her friend.

"I am. I really love it here. Mary Ann's apartment was great, too. There weren't any household problems living in an apartment. I think that is why I kept my place in Fairfield, which I guess I'll give up now that I'm in the house."

Switching topic, she said, "I need your opinion, Simone. I wrote this note to Anthony's mother. I don't hate her. Actually, I feel very sorry for her, given all that's she's been through. Should I send it?"

Simone read it:

Dear Francine,

Although I am no longer involved with your family, I wanted you to know that I genuinely enjoyed your company, and your wonderful cooking. I am sorry things turned out the way they did. No one, especially a mother, should suffer the way you did. I am deeply sorry for what happened to your sons.

You and your husband were always kind and respectful to me, and I will treasure the times we shared together.

Now it is time for me to rebuild my life. I hope you understand that I have no ill feelings toward your family. I just want to be left alone so that I can start over.

Jennifer Keys

Simone read the note, and said, "I think it's lovely. You might want to ask Sid what . . . I need to use the bathroom." Simone charged from the room, and Jennifer could hear Simone vomiting.

"Are you okay, Simone?" Jennifer shouted after her.

Simone emerged from the bathroom, looking pale and feeling woozy.

"Sit down," Jennifer insisted. Goober nuzzled up against her as to say, "Lean on me."

"Thank you. Can you get me some water?"

Jennifer walked to the kitchen, while Goober stood guard watching Simone. He put his head on her lap, and stared his loving eyes into hers.

Simone drank with gusto. "Thanks. I don't know what's gotten into me lately. I must be dehydrated or something. I'm always dizzy, nauseous . . . mornings are worse."

The two women stared at each other. No one spoke the words they were both thinking.

Forty-Nine

The police arrived at the sporting goods store just after it opened for business at nine o'clock. The manager asked if he could be of assistance.

"We need to speak to Carmine Palmieri."

"He's in the back, doing inventory of golfing supplies. I heard on the news about his nephews - really sad."

The policeman didn't utter a word, but walked past the manager, and found Carmine with his head down making notes on a clipboard.

"Carmine Palmieri?"

He looked up, startled to see the cops.

"Is everything okay at my home . . . my wife? What happened to my wife? Oh, my God, was she hit by a car while jogging . . . I told her not to jog in the road." Carmine became anxious.

"Mr. Palmieri, calm down. Your wife, as far as we know, is fine. Please, is there somewhere we can talk?"

Meanwhile, the manager followed closely behind the officers, and announced, "There's a room over here."

"Sir, we need privacy with Mr. Palmieri. If you don't mind, please step outside, away from the door."

The manager left, miffed he wouldn't get the scoop of what was going on.

"What's wrong? Why do you want to talk to me?" Carmine was frightened like he had never been before.

"We're here to ask you where you were two nights ago."

Carmine though. "Let's see . . . oh yeah, I was playing softball at the ball field in Orange. My boss was there. He'd vouch for me." Suddenly, he went pale. "Is this about my nephews?"

"Yes, it is."

"I only saw them at the game. Their family and mine, we don't talk no more. My brother – their father – weaseled me out of my share of the family company. We haven't spoken in years."

He took out a hankie and wiped his brow. "Geez, I thought maybe you thought I hurt those boys. I hate my brother, and all, but I would never do such a thing. It ain't worth going to jail for that family. We mind our business, and we live our separate lives. You know what I mean?"

"Do you have any idea who could have beaten the boys?"

Carmine thought for a while. He ran through his litany of family members, and said, "Nah, nobody I can think of. Those boys were trouble-makers, always playing pranks on people, maybe they pissed somebody off. Did you hear about what they did to that poor girl Jennifer, Anthony's girlfriend? That was terrible."

"Can you vouch for your whereabouts that evening?" the officer asked.

"I played in the game. Afterwards, I showered and went home. Had dinner, fell asleep at some point . . . let me think . . . yeah, I watched Rachael Maddow on MSNBC. I woke up around midnight, and went to bed."

"Was anyone home who could testify to you being home at that time?"

"Yeah, my wife," he lied.

"At any time, did you leave your home, and return a short time later?"

Now Carmine was getting annoyed, and his temper was rising. "Look, I'm telling you, I had nothing to do with those boys' beating. I hope they're okay. They are family, after all."

The officers wrote down his address, home and cell phone numbers, and told him they will be interviewing his wife, and other members of the family.

"Ah, listen," he said. "Don't talk to my daughter, Veronica. She's a little slow, and gets upset real fast. Besides, she's got a baby at home. She can't even take care of herself, much less hurt the boys."

The officers left the room leaving Carmine alone. He speed-dialed his wife and left a voice message. "Hey listen, the cops were here a few minutes ago. They asked me about the night the twins got beaten up. I told them I came home right after the game. I also told them you were there, too."

He hung up the phone, opened the office door, and returned to his task taking inventory.

Fifty

"I have a follow-up appointment with Dr. Brady tomorrow. How about you come with me," Jennifer said, encouraging Simone. "I need a ride, anyway. I'm still not comfortable driving up to New Haven. That is, if you don't mind driving."

"Yes, that'd be fine. I can take you," Simone mumbled, still in shock from her friend's previous question.

"Pregnant? Jen, do you think I could be pregnant? After my accident, I never thought I could ever become pregnant again. I don't know what to do."

"The first thing you have to do, Simone, is get yourself a pregnancy test kit, and go home and talk to Charlie."

"Yes . . . yes . . . you're right. Talk to Charlie." Simone sounded robotic.

"Simone, do you think the Palmieris' think I hurt the twins – or hired someone to hurt them?"

"They believe you're living in a rehabilitation facility, and are not allowed any visitors. The news report said almost every bone in their bodies were broken. It must have been a very strong person to inflect that amount of pain. No, I don't think you're a suspect, Jennifer."

"Good," Jennifer answered."

"Do you have any idea who could have done this to them? It must have been an awful sight. That poor janitor, finding their crumpled bodies," Simone asked.

"I know Carmine always hated his brother," Jennifer said. "I wonder if they'll question him."

"Don't give it a second thought," Simone said comforting her friend. She got up to leave. She hugged Jennifer, told her she thought the note was a lovely gesture, and she was sure Sid wouldn't find any legal reason not to send it. "I'll call you later."

Simone left Jennifer's home, and drove directly to CVS, where she purchased the kit. She shoved the package into her leather messenger bag for added secrecy.

When Charlie arrived home, he found her sitting on the sofa staring out into space.

"Hello, my love." He kissed his wife, and saw how pale she was. "Simone, are you feeling okay?"

"Charlie, I'm pregnant," she blurted out, holding up the pregnancy test strip for him to inspect.

His shock morphed into reality, then turned into the biggest grin Simone had ever seen on her husband's face.

"So why are you looking so dismayed, Simone?"

"I'm frightened, Charlie. I'm deeply frightened that I'll lose this baby, too." She buried her head in his shoulder and sobbed tears of fear and excitement all blending into one emotion.

"Don't be frightened, Simone. I'm here."

Fifty-One

Francine and Johnny spent their days sitting vigil by their son's bedsides. The past two days had been consumed with worry, prayers and questions. They took shifts staying at the hospital. While Francine prayed over her sons, Johnny was home sleeping, or checking in on the company. One of the floor managers stepped up to oversee the day-to-day operations, giving Johnny freedom to spend time at the hospital. When Johnny arrived at the hospital, Francine would return home to sleep, cook and clean.

When they were both at the hospital, they stood by their boy's beds, walked the hallways together, or drank burnt coffee in flimsy Styrofoam cups.

Three nights after the beating, Johnny arrived home at seven. He was tired and hungry. The few meals he ate in the hospital cafeteria were grim. He looked in the refrigerator and discovered that Francine had prepared a meal for him with heating instructions taped to the cover. He realized that although she was consumed by the boys, she still took care of him. *She's a pain in the ass, but really is a good woman,* he admitted.

As he stood by the microwave waiting for his dinner to heat, he glanced to his left and noticed the baby monitor. *What the hell,* he thought, *why not listen in?* He turned on the machine.

"Tara, we have to talk," Carmine was saying, "about the cops coming to my job today, asking questions about Vinny and Anthony."

Johnny shut off the microwave, pulled up a chair, and listened in on his brother's conversation.

"Yeah, so?" Tara asked, placing a plate of veal cutlet and salad in front of him. "I got your voice mail message."

"They asked where I was the other night . . . the night the boys got beaten up. I told them I came home after the game."

"Yeah, you said so in your message."

"I saw you," Carmine said flatly.

"You saw me? Where?"

"At the ballgame."

"I don't know what you're talking about, Carmine," Tara said suddenly feeling trapped. "I went to Veronica's, then came home. You were snoring in the reclining chair. Then I went to bed."

"Don't lie, Tara. I know what you did. I saw you at the game, and couldn't figure out why, so I followed you. You changed your clothes in the back-seat of the car. You wore one of those get ups Muslim women wear. You beat those boys with one of my bats. I saw you, and I heard you shout our family's names, and Jennifer's, too."

She sat down. "So?"

"So? That's all you've got to say?"

"Yeah. Well, what do you want me to do, confess? I gave them what they deserved."

"You didn't have to do what you did, Tara. If the cops find out, you could go to jail for the rest of your life."

She snickered. "And you'll go with me as an accomplice since you saw me, and didn't do anything to stop me. Touché."

"Shit."

"Look," she said calmly, "just act like nothing happened. We heard about the beatings. The boys will live. I should have taken them out when I had the chance."

"Tara!" Carmine snapped. "I can't believe you're saying that. Sure, they messed up our family, but that didn't give you the right to beat them like you did."

"Someone had to stop them, Carmine. They would have continued getting away hurting people. It had to stop. Just keep your mouth shut. If the cops ask you anything again, you tell them what you said at work. Keep your story straight."

"Did they talk to you?"

"Yeah, I told them I went for a run . . . didn't see anyone . . . heard about the tragedy on the news the next day. Sad for the family. Told the cops we ain't talked to them in years, hardly ever see them, and we mind our own business."

"Did they ask about me?"

She paused for enough time to increase Carmine's heartbeat.

"Yeah. I told them you came home after the game, ate some leftovers, and fell asleep watching TV. Funny, they asked me what show you were watching. I thought that was odd."

"What did you tell them?" Carmine asked, remembering what he had told the officers.

"I said you were watching a show on MSNBC. I left you snoring, and went to sleep."

"Good," he said, then added, "I hope those boys make it."

"You're a wuss, Carmine. You don't have the balls to stand up for anything those boys do. Do you know they sexually assaulted Veronica one time while Francine was watching them?"

"What?" Carmine screamed. "You never told me."

"You were too busy wheeling and dealing at your father's company. Anytime I brought up the subject of child rearing you told me you didn't want to hear about it. Fortunately, they didn't rape her, just felt her up, but it permanently traumatized her."

"You should have told me," her husband said.

"And what would you have done about it? Go over there and beat up the boys? They were kids playing doctor, and your daughter was the patient. It was years ago, but it's shit like that, and the attempted rape of that girl in high school when they were teenagers, and then Jennifer. When was it going to stop? When?"

"I'll tell you when it's going to stop," said the voice on the monitor.

Fifty-Two

The doctors at the hospital explained to the twin's parents, "Mr. and Mrs. Palmieri, you must prepare yourselves. The boys have a thirty percent chance of surviving the beatings. Since Anthony is on life support, his survival rate is lower. If they do make it, there is a chance they'll be vegetables. We've seen miracles, but they might need medical care for years to come. In any case, their lives will be very different."

The second surgeon added, "Both will face dozens of future surgeries to repair broken bones, plastic surgery to put their faces back together, and they would be in full body casts for months. After leaving the hospital, they'll have to live in a rehabilitation facility for a minimum of two months."

He continued, "Of course, the police wanted to ask the boys questions about the beatings. Unfortunately, both are in medically-induced comas from the bleeding on their brains, so the police could not get any information from them."

Johnny and Francine nodded taking in what the doctors were saying. Meanwhile, machines beeped and buzzed around the boys. Bags of fluids and tubes extended beneath and over their bedsheets. Medical devices covered them, keeping them alive. Looking at them in this state, it was impossible to tell them apart.

Vigils, prayers, masses, novenas, Rosaries, and candles were lit for the twins. There was a steady stream of relatives that came to the hospital to pay their respects. Although Carmine fought Tara for days, he acquiesced and agreed to go to the hospital. "After all, Carmine, it wasn't the boys who took the business away from you, it was their father."

"I guess, but I don't want to talk to Johnny or his wife."

"We'll just stay as long as they'll allow us to. No more," Tara assured him.

At the hospital, Johnny and Francine sat in the waiting room, while other relatives went in to say a prayer, or send healing energy to the boys. Sobs were heard over the beeps, alarms and breathing machines.

"Look who just walked in," Francine whispered to her husband. "It's your brother and Tara."

"What the hell does he want?" Johnny said angrily.

"Be nice. It had to take a lot for them to come here," Francine said.

Tara and Carmine saw the couple in the waiting room, walked past them, and stopped at the nurses' station. A nurse directed them to ICU, in an open area where they were watched by nurses and doctors twenty-four hours a day.

Tara made the sign of the cross. They turned, and headed towards the elevator. As they walked past the waiting room, Francine saw Tara wipe away tears.

"Hypocrites," Johnny mumbled to Francine.

After three weeks in the hospital, Vinny was the first one to show any signs of improvement. An investigating detective asked Vinny, "Do you know who did this?"

"Don't know," Vinny mumbled.

"Was it a man, or a woman?" the detective asked.

"Don't know."

"Did you see their face?"

"No."

"Did they say anything?"

"Can't remember."

The doctor cut off further questions. "They need to continue to heal. Maybe in another week or so, they'll be able to give you some solid information. Until then, please refrain from more questions. I'll call you if I think either boy shows signs he's up for talking."

Fifty-Three

Since Simone received the results three months ago that she was pregnant with twins, she hadn't been able to focus on anything else. She had to force herself to concentrate on work, especially the upcoming weddings scheduled for that year. The celebrity chef's wedding was scheduled for Mother's Day, Judy Smith's wedding was the following weekend on May nineteenth, and the Lee wedding was scheduled for October, nine months away.

The babies weren't due for another five months, but the doctor warned her that they might not go full term. Simone's anxiety level was increasing thinking about all that had to be done both at work and in preparation of the new arrivals.

Charlie was a tremendous help taking over the household chores of food shopping, cleaning, laundry, and preparing most meals. Although Simone loved to cook, by the end of the day she was often too exhausted to think about dinner.

One Friday evening, Simone was cleaning out a dresser in the sitting room attached to the master bedroom, which will be used as a nursery. She reflected back on what caused the overhaul of the rooms, and thought, *How a miracle hides within the walls of a tragedy.*

While cleaning out one of the drawers, her fingers landed on a broken coin. She lifted it up, and a flood of memories and emotions burst forth. In her palm was a Mizpah Coin she and her mother shared.

"Alison-Simone," her mother had said, "keep this half of the coin with you. I will hold the other half. Know that I am with you at all times, no matter how far apart we are."

Those were some of the last words her mother had spoken to Simone the day before Simone left Louisville, Kentucky to start college at New York University. After her mother's death, Simone found half of the coin tucked in the change purse of her mother's pocketbook.

Simone held the two coin pieces together and read:

Simone recalled the history behind the coin. Her mother told her that according to the Bible, Jacob left the house of his father-in-law, Laban, in the middle of the night taking with him animals, Laban's wives, children and grandchildren. Laban searched for Jacob, and when he found him, the two formalized their separation. The two men erected a pile of stones, called a mizpah. They agreed this tower was a border between them, not to pass, or to do evil.

The mizpah has come to represent an emotional bond between people who are separated, either geographically or by death. It is also referred to as the name of a cemetery, and can be found on headstones and other memorials.

Simone's thoughts turned to Jennifer, and her love of the cairns at Silver Sands Beach. The stones were like "a rock cemetery" she had said. They were her mizpah.

Simone wished her mother was alive to see her now, a married woman, with twins on the way. She was a successful wedding planner running a multi-million dollar business. This final realization caused her to pause. *What was she going to do after the babies were born?* How would she possibly go back to work?

She decided that when Charlie got home, they would discuss child care, but right now, exhaustion and swollen ankles forced her to sit down and relax. Soon she was dozing in her reclining chair.

"Simone, wake up," Charlie said softly as he gently shook his wife. "It's six o'clock."

"Oh my. I've been asleep for over two hours."

"I guess you needed the sleep. Are you hungry, my love? I brought home crab cakes from DaPietro."

Simone yawned as she waddled to the dining room table. "Oh, Charlie," she said excitedly, "I found the Mizpah Coin my mother gave me when I left for college." She took it out of her pocket and showed the charm to Charlie. She explained the Bible story to him, and how she would hold her half of the charm in her hand whenever she missed her mother. She included her thoughts about Jennifer, and how the cairns were like her mizpah.

"That's a beautiful sentiment," Charlie said observing the charm.

"I want to save the charm for when our babies are older. I'd like to gift them each a half, so they will always be connected."

After dinner Simone fixed a cup of ginger tea, her new coffee alternative. Unfortunately, her consumption of four to five cups of coffee a day was reduced to two cups, according to doctor's orders. She found the ginger helped with morning sickness, and with a few drops of honey, and a great imagination, she could pretend she was drinking coffee.

"Charlie," Simone said as she settled herself on the sofa, "We need to discuss child care. I guess I never really gave it much thought, but what am I going to do about my company? Should we start to interview nannies?"

"There are several women who work at the hotel who babysit their grandchildren" Charlie said. "Maybe we could ask one of them if they would be interested, or maybe they know someone who would."

"That's a great idea, but I'd like to give it some thought. I have another idea, Charlie, but I don't know how you'd feel about it."

"Is this a 'we need to talk' conversation?" he teased.

"Yes, as a matter of fact, it is," Simone said seriously. "You know that because I've lived on my own for so many years as a widow, I'm very independent."

Charlie chuckled, "Really? I hadn't noticed," he said sarcastically.

"Be serious," she said as she tossed a pillow at him. "It's been an issue with us, and you can't deny it. I've often made decisions on my own before consulting with you. But now that we're married, I have to stop myself from making rash, impromptu decisions. Like buying Jennifer's house. I didn't consult with you first, and I apologize."

"Simone," Charlie said sitting down next to his wife and holding her hand, "that was a great decision. To the point, though, we do need to discuss major decisions."

"I have an idea, but there are several moving parts. . . ." Her words trailed off. "I'm exhausted Charlie. I need to go to bed, and mull over my thoughts."

"Okay, my love. Whatever it is you're thinking, I'm sure it'll be a great idea."

I just need everyone involved to agree, she thought, as she headed off to bed.

Fifty-Four

It was an unusually warm February Saturday afternoon. The staff at "I Do" were working two small weddings, while Simone was at home resting. The doctor told her to stick with desk work, and to avoid standing on her feet all day. Her staff was competent and she was only a phone call away.

She and Charlie sat on the deck, reading the newspaper, dressed in heavy Irish knit sweaters and drinking hot tea.

Simone's neighbor Cynthia was walking her dog, and shouted, "Good morning. How are you feeling, Simone?"

"Great," Simone said waving.

"May I come up to talk?" Cynthia asked. "And bring Grendel along too?"

"Of course," Charlie and Simone answered simultaneously.

Grendel was a one hundred pound Rottweiler, known by the neighbors as the sweetest and most affectionate gentle giant in Westport. He gave the couple's hands licks, and energetically wagged his stub of a tail.

"I wanted to tell you that we are going to sell our home and move to Raleigh, North Carolina. Brett's company is moving its headquarters there; they made him a fantastic offer."

"Oh, no," Simone said. Cynthia was one of the first people to welcome her to Westport. In fact, it was at a cookout, hosted by Cynthhia and Brett, where Simone had met Pete Cody, the contractor who did her home renovations.

"We're thinking of putting the house on the market in early April. We're going down next weekend to look at homes. Brett's job begins in March, so he'll be commuting until we sell the house, and move. We are also going to sell all the furniture in the house. I want to start anew. Besides, my beachy décor won't work. I'm going to miss the beach, Simone. I dread the thought of being landlocked, hours away from the coast. But, if Brett can hang in there for another decade, or so, we'll move to Florida."

"It sounds as if you've got it all planned out. It's wonderful to hear. But I'm going to miss you."

"We'll miss you too, Simone. By the way, if you know of anyone who might be interested in buying the house, let me know."

Without skipping a beat, Simone raised her hand and shouted, "I do!"

She quickly continued, "I mean, I might know someone who would be interested in buying your house and the furniture. So before you sign up with a realtor, please give me a few days, and I'll get back to you."

After Cynthia and Grendel left, Charlie asked, "Who do you think would buy Cynthia's house?"

Simone's smile reached her eyes.

"I know that smile so well, my love. What are you up to?"

"Remember we discussed child care for the babies? How about I buy Cynthia's house, and move Mrs. Smith and Irene up to Westport. They can live in the house, and be our nannies. Judy said that since her father passed away, her mother never does anything except sit on the porch all day and stare out at the mountains. This would give her, and Irene a reason for getting up in the mornings," Simone said eagerly.

"Do you think Mrs. Smith would consider this offer?" Charlie asked. "After all, it is a big request. And, do you really think Mrs. Smith would accept you purchasing the house? She's a very proud woman."

"Charlie, Mr. Smith gave me a penthouse apartment in Paris. Here's an opportunity for me to give back to them. They took me in year after year, and never asked for any monetary payment. And, I have a substantial amount of money from my parent's estate, Joe's estate, and from the lawsuit against the taxi company. Plus the money I make organizing weddings. I'm not hurting financially. I'm going to rephrase that – *we're* not hurting for money. What use is having millions if you can't help others?"

"Talk to Judy, and see what she thinks," Charlie said. "But don't get your hopes up in case Mrs. Smith doesn't want to move north."

"I'm so excited, Charlie. To think, we'd have family taking care of our babies."

"My love," Charlie said, holding his wife's hand, "I agree. We've been very fortunate, and you've been very generous. I think buying Cynthia's house could work for all of us. I hope Mrs. Smith agrees. Let's call Judy now and tell her your plan."

Epilogue

Jennifer was back living in the Woodmont house on the beach. Goober returned for a few refresher dog obedience classes, and continued to be a loyal and constant companion.

Jennifer returned as a part-time wedding planner to "I Do". Goober had a dog bed under her desk, and others in the office loved the added members to the team.

Cindy Hom welcomed Jennifer with a gentle hug, "You have an amazing reputation," she said.

"Thanks," Jennifer said. "I've heard great things about you, as well," she fibbed. It was a white lie, Jennifer decided. Simone had asked Jennifer to play referee between Cindy and GG. After a week, she understood Simone's concerns about the two of them. Jennifer had a game plan in her head she was sure was going to work.

"No dog biscuits, or people food," Jennifer told her co-workers. "When Goober is wearing his vest, he is working."

The Lee wedding plans were proceeding nicely. GG had created sketches of how he envisioned the décor of the venue in Great Neck, Long Island. The Lee family was pleased with the layout, design, and overall structure of the wedding. But they passed on the idea of the flying veil.

"Cindy, is it customary for the bride not to have any input in the wedding?" Simone asked her. "I never met her. Have you?"

"Yes, I did on one of my trips to the Lee's apartment. She was there. She's tiny, very timid, and agreed to everything the groom's grandparents presented. I have a feeling this was an arranged marriage, but the Lees aren't admitting to that theory."

Mary Ann and Greg's apartment was always available to Jennifer if she ever felt she wanted to go back to apartment living. They'd welcome a house sitter anytime.

* * * * *

Tara finally convinced Carmine to move to another town, away from his brother next door. They sold their house, and bought a condo in Heritage Hills in Somers, New York. It was a commute for Carmine, but he didn't mind. It was that much less time he'd have to be home, listening to Tara's nagging. It also got them further away from Veronica and her marital problems.

The semi-attached home was in a fifty-five plus community with twenty-six hundred units that ranged from one-bedroom to multiple bedroom units. There were daily activities, a state of the art fitness gym, golf course, pickle ball courts, shuttle buses, and upscale shopping and restaurants only a short drive away.

"I hate to say it, Tara, you were right. We should have done this years ago."

The sale of their house closed in the morning, and the purchase of their condo followed in the afternoon. All their possessions were loaded on the moving van, ready for their new adventure.

Everything went smoothly, and while the men unloaded the van in Somers, Tara offered to buy lunch for everyone at DeCicco's, a new gourmet supermarket that had everything from homemade cannoli to prepared foods, sandwiches, wine, and a lovely outdoor patio where one could get table service while watching the sunset.

She got in her car and headed down the three mile hill to the market. The winding road twisted and turned, with sharp hairpin curves. *This isn't great for senior citizens living here. I hope they clear this road when it snows,* Tara thought.

Suddenly, and without any advanced warning, Tara's brakes gave way. There was no stopping the car, it careened out of control, tires squealing on the tight turns, her body rocked back and forth in time to the turns. She pumped the brakes vigorously, but there was nothing behind the pedal, only the car's floor. She screamed as the vehicle slammed into a boulder, flipped over, and slid another two hundred feet before crashing into two oncoming cars, then coming to a sudden stop.

The other drivers and their passengers got out of their cars, just in time before Tara's car burst into flames, killing the screaming woman trapped inside. And destroying all evidence.

* * * * *

Johnny and Francine were in the kitchen. He sat at the table reading the box scores while she cleaned vegetables. The phone rang.

"Hello," Johnny said, picking up the phone.

The person on the other end identified himself as being from the Somers Police Department.

"I'm sorry to inform you that Tara Palmieri died in a car accident this afternoon. Her husband Carmine noted you as next of kin, requesting your help during this extremely difficult time," said the voice on the phone. Carmine listened as the officer provided details.

"What a tragedy," Johnny told the officer. "I'm sorry to hear this news. Thank you for notifying me. We haven't spoken to them in many years. We saw they had their house for sale, but we never knew that the house was sold, or where they had moved to."

Another pause as he listened.

"Well," Johnny continued, "I'm sorry to say, there's nothing we can do to help. You see, we have our two sons living with us now. We are their caretakers. They need twenty-four hour care, so between me and my wife, plus visiting nurses, physical therapist, and doctors, we couldn't possibly find time. Please extend our sympathies to the family."

Johnny hung up the phone, and looked at his wife, who by now, had shut off the water and listened to the conversation. They stared at each other. No words spoken.

Francine turned back to the sink, and continued cleaning the broccoli rabe. Johnny went back to reading the sports section.

"When you have a chance Francine, throw out that baby monitor. We don't need it no more."

Yes, in the Palmieri Family, secrets were sacred.